Thirty Days, Thirty Stories:
An Anthology of Shorts

Edited by Renee Schnebelin

To Mike,
Thank you for your
support!
All the best,
Renee Schn—

www.reneeschnebelinbooks.com

Purple Elephant Publishing

D1526994

Anthology Thirty Days, Thirty Stories (Volume One)
Anthology Authors

ISBN-13: 9798698342120

Library of Congress Control Number: 2018675309
Printed in the United States of America

Contents

Part Two: Murders and Mysteries

Part Three: Loves and Losses

Part Four: Fantasies and Majicks

Part Five: Ups and Downs

Part Six: Artifices and Realities

Part Seven: 24 Twenty-Four Word Stories

Part Eight: Anything Goes

The Contributors

A Note from the Editor:

Where do I begin? At the beginning I suppose.

Writing and organizing this Anthology began after thirty days of feverishly writing thirty short stories, which were prompted by an amazing organization: The Literal Challenge.

I have had becoming a published author on my bucket list since grade school and I am about to be able to cross that one off. I also have two other novels in the works that I hope to publish before year's end as well, 'Dream Walker', and 'The Alexia Chronicles.'

However, this Anthology is my prime focus as I have thirteen other author's counting on me to share their works with the world. And that is what I intend to do.

So, without further ado turn the page and Samia will give you a quick, 'what you will encounter' within this book. - Renee Schnebelin

What You Will Encounter...

Perhaps the first thing you will notice about the contents of this book is that there are quite a few more than the thirty stories indicated by the title. What you have before you is not false advertising. These stories, written by a bunch of complete strangers to each other, are the product of a challenge we all entered to keep us writing in various and interesting ways. Every day of the month of June in the thick of the 2020 pandemic, we were provided with a brief for what to write and had 36 hours in which to write and submit it. Over those thirty days, we were to produce thirty unique stories each, sometimes with minutes to spare, sometimes on little sleep, sometimes on the edge of sanity, but always running with the bit, exercising whatever raw skill we could harness.

The authors contained herein come from various countries, and you will see this reflected in the settings, language, and alternative spellings. If there is one thing you can expect from reading these stories, it is to be transported far beyond where you are now.

This collection contains an assortment of stories from these authors over the thirty days. Then there are the bonus stories, and an entire chapter dedicated to stories that are only 24 words long and starting with the phrase *One day...*

One day, I picked up a random book of short stories to read. The stories made me chuckle, think, fear, hope, cry ... and learn. - Samia Nicolas

Part One: Thrills and Spills

Darkness

What happens when they come at night,
All draped in black with no sign of light?

Frightened and all alone,
I sit up in fear at the sound of the moan.

Where is that noise coming from?
Maybe just the sound of a hum?

Why won't they leave me be?
They must know that I cannot see.

I hear it again, so I sit up in bed,
I can see the faint outline of someone's head.

Why oh why won't they leave me alone?
They must know that I am prone.

- R. Schnebelin

The Orchid

***

Renee Schnebelin

She saw him....

Dark brown hair, hazel eyes, incredible smile. He was wearing khaki shorts and a button-down black shirt. She watched as he made his way towards her. As he sat down across the table, she said hello. That was how it began. He smiled.

"Are y'all ready to order?" The waitress snapped them out of the trance they were in, bringing them back to reality. They had decided to meet for lunch on a whim after meeting in a chat group on Twitter. He asked and she accepted. That was yesterday.

"I'm sorry, we haven't even had a chance to look at the menu, but we will take two waters please." She said as she let her gaze drift back to the handsome gentleman that sat across the table from her. "Thank you for asking me to lunch."

"Thank you for saying yes," He said as he shifted nervously in his seat.

Their conversation continued on for the next few hours and seemed to flow smoothly. After lunch they walked through the park hand in hand.

She could feel the butterflies building up in her stomach when he asked what she would be doing for dinner. She told him that she planned on making spaghetti with garlic toast and asked if he would like to join her. He obliged.

"No funny business I promise." He squeezed her hand.

"It never even crossed my mind." She squeezed back and giggled.

She almost couldn't believe that the date was going this well.

As they walked past a flower shop, she mentioned how she loved to buy flowers. She mentioned that this shop had the best Orchids. He said that every potted plant he had ever purchased had died. She laughed and squeezed his hand tight.

They walked that way all the way back to her quaint little cottage that sat back from the road a bit. He noted how beautiful and serene the lot was. She had purchased the home for that very reason. The privacy.

She pulled her keys out of her purse, unlocked the door, and opened it. She let him walk in first and locked the door behind them as they entered the spacious living room. The cottage was professionally decorated and immaculate. Filled with only fine pieces, hand-picked and shipped in from around the world. The purple elephant riding a bike was her favorite and was a gift from her first love, Andrew. He had bought it for her on their first date at the coffee shop.

"Sit wherever you like. Make yourself at home and I can grab us something to drink. Wine or a beer?" She said as she headed for the kitchen.

"Red wine, if you have it." He said as he took a seat in the chair that ben had purchased for her while they were backpacking through Europe. Ben was her longest relationship, one that she almost married; but the wedding ended up getting postponed after ben became ill.

She headed into the kitchen and pulled the special bottle of red down from the shelf, poured him a glass, and smiled. She poured herself a glass of white and carried the two drinks out to the living room, handing him the glass as she passed by.

"That painting is amazing." He said pointing to the mural that hung above the couch. It had two red bicycles in the center, both had a basket, and a bell. Nothing more, nothing less. It wasn't her favourite piece; Cal had it made specifically for her after finding out that she loved bicycle art. Cal was her third love, which only spanned a week, but she fell in love hard with him and even cried a bit when she had to let him go.

"This wine is making me sleepy." He said with a yawn. He closed his eyes.

She began to count as his chest rose and fell. It wouldn't take long for the poison to take hold. She smiled at the thought. David had no idea that this would be his last date. She knew that this one wouldn't last long because he didn't buy her an Orchid.

Whiskers

***

Robert Graver

A young boy, no older than eight, lay upon a blanket of grass, wearing nothing but his underwear. He was surrounded by a ring of dismembered limbs of small animals, blood smeared across his chest, his hands stained a dark red hue. A woman screamed, her ear-piercing shriek cutting through the silence of an otherwise peaceful morning. The lady ran out of her house, into the garden, to be met by the morbid and grizzly scene before her. Her son, John Smith, smiled. It was an evil grin, devoid of any sympathy or emotion.

John had always been a quiet child; keeping to himself in school, getting good grades, he was a normal kid. He had charm and charisma, a nice group of friends. What turned him into the child that scared his mother to the core, the child that could do such unspeakable things, so nonchalantly? Any sign of enthusiasm, anxiety, or interest was gone, as if his brain lacked the ability to have any form of rationality or remorse. John's mother, Cindy Smith, needed to do something, and fast. This wasn't the first time she had found John in this predicament.

It had begun almost two years ago when his father left. He showed no emotions towards his parents' break up. He didn't cry; he didn't ask why his dad was gone and not coming back. He just continued on with his life as though nothing had happened. He kept his homework up to date, his bedroom tidy, and ate all his vegetables. It seemed as though nothing had changed for John. The first time Cindy found her son lying almost naked, was a month after the breakup. It was by no means as dramatic or harrowing as this morning's scene, but it was still disturbing, nonetheless.

John had a fascination with bugs. He would always catch as many as he could during the weekend; and each Sunday, before going back to school, he would release all but his favourite from the collection he made. He would take the specimen jar to school and share his find with the class. Nothing odd, just a child who loved insects.

Cindy's separation took place over the summer holidays, so John had been collecting a surprising amount over the six week period off school. Instead of releasing his collection each weekend, he had kept them all. He had separate boxes and jars for each species he found, and a notebook full of descriptions and oddities about the various creatures. Probably due to his overactive imagination, or lack of stimulation during the holidays, he began to conduct experiments on the bugs.

It began with simple 'fights': which bug was stronger, who would win. It was typical child's play really. He was interested in nothing more than which insect would come out on top. It escalated quite a fair amount after these fights. John would sneak into his mother's bathroom and steal her tweezers, using them as tiny operating tools on the bugs. The flying ants had their wings torn off. The stag beetles' pincers were removed. The worms were dissected into three distinct segments. The amount of precision and dedication John had whilst performing these experiments was quite a feat. The largest, or most intrinsic, performance would have to be when he found a centipede. Each leg was individually removed, picked off one by one with the tweezers, and kept aside for who knew what purpose.

When Cindy walked into John's bedroom, she found him lying there, a smile on his face. This was the only time she had seen him smile or have any kind of emotion since his father left. He was wearing his underwear, and each box and jar of bugs was decanted onto the bed around him, forming a messy circle of insect carcasses around her son. Maybe it was just part of one of his weird experiments, she told herself. It was just a phase: he was acting out because his father left. Cindy brushed it off as just a blip in his life.

It wasn't until their house cat, Whiskers, went missing that Cindy began to suspect more than a morbid fascination for the dead from her son. When confronted about the cat's disappearance, he denied knowing anything about it. Cats were cats. It was probably off hunting, or sleeping somewhere out of sight. Cindy accepted the fact that John was probably right, but she had no clue that her son was responsible for the poor feline's demise.

John's father had a small allotment plot, not far from where John attended school. One Friday evening, on his way home, Whiskers began to follow John home, jumping onto a wall and pacing alongside him. Not too far from the allotment, John scooped the cat up and headed through the gates of the gardeners' paradise. Quickly finding his father's plot, he began to rummage through his school bag, searching for something. Shoving books aside, he finally found the key he was looking for. The key unlocked the padlock on the small shed at the top of the plot: housing for any tools and equipment needed for tending to the vegetables and plants.

Briefly checking that no one was around, John snuck in, locking the door behind him. He put Whiskers down, a soft purr coming from the tabby. He began to rummage through the tools on the bench, until he found a pair of pliers. He started slowly: gripping the tool in his hand, and the cat in his other, he gradually plucked each whisker from the cat's face. There was a small hiss and a struggle with each pluck. By the time Whiskers had no whiskers, John's arms were covered in bloody scratches, his school jumper ripped up the arms. Deciding he could easily pass the scratches off as getting into a fight at school, or taking a shortcut home through the thorn bushes perhaps, he knew his mother wouldn't suspect anything.

He found a small leather belt, some string, and a pair of secateurs scattered around the shed, placing each item in a specific order on the bench. He picked the cat up again, embracing himself for the scratches that would come. Quickly using the belt and string, he hogtied the cat's legs together, bound it to the table with the belt, and picked up the secateurs. With the cat in place, he snipped its tail off. One clean motion; an easy operation. The cat screamed out in pain, hissing, trying to wiggle its way free. The poor mammal gave up, exhausted, almost accepting its fate. Anyway, cats had nine lives, right? At least that was how John saw it. One life for all its whiskers; one life for the tail. Another four for each limb, one for the head... but that had to be last. There were still another two lives to use up.

John thought back to when Whiskers was a kitten and almost got hit by a truck; that could count as one life. The other life, he decided, was when the stupid animal fell in the bath and almost drowned. Good. Each limb, and finally the head would use all nine lives up.

John continued on his sadistic endeavour. The legs proved to be a bit more difficult to remove than the tail. The bone and sinews, tougher, especially when the blades were blunt. After the first leg finally came off, he searched around the room for something better. A small scalpel - not big enough. Pruning secateurs - again, not strong enough for the task. John finally found a small hacksaw, probably used to remove tougher branches and roots, or stalks from stubborn plants. This would work.

John set back to his task, removing each leg, placing them neatly side by side on the bench. Whiskers had probably passed out due to the pain after the first leg, but there was still a pulse. John could feel the faint beating beneath his fingers as he caressed the fur, all matted and bloody. Finally, after a deep breath, he began to take the head off. Whiskers' final life, gone. The cat was finally at rest after the torturous medical procedure it had endured.

John picked up each limb and began to place them around the floor, laying them into a circle. The head was placed at the top, and the whiskers scattered around the centre. The limp body was left clamped to the bench. John removed all his clothes, minus his underwear, and lay down in the centre of the circle, breathing deeply, smiling.

After five minutes of resting there, John got up and gathered all the dismembered limbs and the body, and swept the whiskers into a neat pile. He put all the tools back, carefully making sure they were how he found them. John grabbed a small potato sack from behind the door, stuffing Whiskers and his limbs inside. Peering out of the window, making sure the allotment was still empty, John unlocked the door, grabbing a shovel on the way out, and proceeded to bury the cat in his father's allotment.

He headed home, stopping by the local store to buy a lollipop. As he stepped through the front door, Cindy rushed over, concerned at the state of his uniform and the scratches on his arm.

"I'm fine. Just took a detour home. Didn't realise there were so many thorn bushes though," John sucked on the sweet, pulling it out of his mouth, admiring how much he had left to go.

The next available appointment that Doctor Wells had was on Tuesday the following week. Cindy booked the day off work and pulled John from school - a stomach bug, she told them. They arrived at the office at eleven, their appointment not being for another half hour. Cindy was always so anal about being on time; always early, almost too early, the majority of the time. Today was no different. She and John sat in the waiting room until the receptionist called them through.

Doctor Wells, in her late forties, a few grey hairs creeping through her auburn hair, greeted them at the door.

"Come in Mrs. Smith," she bent down, looking at John, "and you must be John."

Wells offered them a seat on a large, leather couch against one wall, opposite a desk. The rest of the room was laid out meticulously - as if someone had seen too many movies of what a therapist's office should look like.

A single chaise lounge chair lurked beneath the bay window. He could see a small bonsai tree, a minimalistic fish tank and three framed certificates on the wall above the desk. Wells had graduated from Harvard State with a PhD in Cognitive Behavioural Therapy, her masters in Child and Adolescent Psychotherapy. Her doctorate in Child and Adolescent Psychoanalytic. It had taken a truly remarkable amount of experience and study to get to where she was in her field.

"Can I offer you a drink, Mrs. Smith?"

"Miss. It's just Miss Smith, and no thanks, I'm fine," Cindy replied, already making it clear to Doctor Wells that there was no father figure involved.

"Alright, shall we begin? If you feel comfortable, John, could you sit on the chair by the window for me?"

John obeyed, placing himself down gently on the soft cushions, wiggling around to get comfortable.

"Good, now I'm going to ask your mother a series of questions, so I can begin to understand and help diagnose you, okay?"

John nodded.

Wells began to write on her notepad, four distinct headings: interpersonal, affective, lifestyle and anti-social.

"Okay, Cindy, can you tell me if your son displays any of the following characteristics. Glibness, superficial charm, grandiosity, pathological lying and manipulation of others?"

Cindy sat silently for a moment, gathering her thoughts.

"He can be very charming; he has a lot of friends at school who all speak highly of him. They praise him for being caring and knowing everything they like. I wouldn't say he is a liar, though."

Wells made a few scribbles on her page.

"All right, has it ever crossed your mind that John could be putting on a false act for his friends? You mentioned that he knows everything they like, and he cares for them. Do you know if his friends see him as a leader, someone they follow everywhere, and would do whatever he asked?"

"Well...sure. They were all at our house for his eighth birthday earlier in the year, and I vaguely remember him asking each of his friends to go and get specific items from around the house. My personal belongings, mainly, and some generic household items. Some of his friends were dubious, not wanting to be caught stealing, but he was able to convince them, somehow." Cindy patted her eyes with a tissue, pushing a tear back.

"Thank you, it would seem that manipulation and charm are definite characteristics at the moment. It would also seem that through those actions, he is displaying impulsive, stimulation-seeking behaviour." Wells put a few words under the lifestyle heading.

"Now, when these children stole the items he was asking for, did you confront them, and John about what they were taking?"

Cindy nodded in response.

"Did John take responsibility for these actions? Was he sorry for asking others to steal for him?"

"Not really. He didn't say he was sorry, he just said it was their idea. He tried to blame his friends. He didn't seem to care that they were caught either."

Wells passed a box of tissues across the table to Cindy.

"Thank you. I think I have everything I need for this part of the session. It would seem that your son is displaying all four features of psychopathic behaviour. He has displayed lack of empathy through impulsive and criminal activity, no sign of remorse for those actions, all while being manipulative and controlling of others through lying and superficial charm to achieve what he wants. Now, there are two methods I can use to proceed from here. I can continue with the PCL-R test, asking you and John another sixteen or so questions, rating them between zero and three. Each question's response adds up to a total of forty. Anything between thirty and forty would clinically diagnose John as having a psychopathic condition. Or, I can schedule you in for another session and begin some cognitive behavioural therapy with John, helping him talk about what goes on in his mind, and how the physical actions and his thoughts are connected, and how we can change this, getting him out of this vicious cycle," Wells waited for Cindy's response.

Cindy looked over towards her son, sitting

quietly, taking everything in. Did he understand everything that was being said? Perhaps all these official terms and use of more sophisticated language would be too advanced for him to understand.

He just sat there, staring blankly at the wall. This reaction, or lack of from her son made her mind up for her.

"I'd like to have another session, Doctor Wells. Please help my boy," she was almost pleading, crying out for help: a desperate mother, wanting what was best for her son.

They Were

***

Renee Schnebelin

The view was amazing....

She stood at the edge of the lake mesmerized by its stillness. It was almost as if the surface had turned to glass, inviting her to walk across to the other side where the tall grasses stood waist-high, filled with crickets and frogs. At least that is what Olivia imagined lived in the tall grasses that were unreachable unless you swam across.

Today seemed to be one of those days where anything seemed possible: maybe she would finally finish that novel she had been writing; for what seemed like years, or perhaps she would land that dream job she had been chasing for months. Olivia smiled at the thought of either of those things occurring and breathed in the sweet summer air. Just standing there, dreaming, and imagining how great it would feel to achieve just one of those dreams.

Those beautiful thoughts came to a halt just as someone pushed her forward, causing her to lose her balance and falling into the pond. Time slowed down as she fell forward, opening her eyes just as her face touched the still surface. Letting gravity take over, she stopped struggling and just let herself be fully absorbed by the water, slowly sinking to the bottom where she held her breath for a moment, then pushing off the mossy rocks, sending her back up above the surface. She opened her eyes and came face to face with...

"OLIVER!" She screamed while attempting to splash him.

Oliver was her snotty-nosed little brother, always sneaking up on her when she was trying to meditate, trying to write, trying to use the bathroom. He was ten years younger than she was, which meant when Mom and Dad were out of town, which was all the time, she was in charge.

Oliver had turned thirteen this year and Olivia just graduated from college and had moved back home. Mom and Dad took that as the perfect opportunity to do all the traveling they had missed out on the last twenty-three years. They were always quick to remind her of all the times they had to say no to a vacation because of her and Oliver. She was always quick to remind them that they could have taken their children with them or allowed her and Oliver to go away to summer camp. Instead, they chose to just complain about the existence of their children.

Oliver stood at the edge of the pond and laughed. "Couldn't have timed that more perfectly. Also, are you going to make dinner?"

Shit! It must be getting late. She had promised to make him spaghetti tonight and bake a cake for his birthday, which was today. Shit! Oliver might be a brat, but he was still her brother and she would do anything to make him smile, keep him safe, and make him feel loved.

She stood and walked to the pond's edge, grabbing Oliver's hand, and hoisting herself out onto the grass. "Sorry for losing track of time. I was thinking about the novel and about the job and didn't realize how late it had gotten. Ready for spaghetti?"

"Yesss. I am starving." Oliver said, linking his arm through hers. "Thank you, Sis."

The two of them walked arm in arm weaving in and out of the tall oak trees, making their way up to their small red cottage. Dinner tonight would be special, she would make sure of that.

The Storm

It came in so suddenly...

Dinner was lovely and Olivia had just tucked Oliver into bed and closed his bedroom door. She had planned to do the dishes when the winds outside began to howl, the thunder boomed and lightning lit up the dark sky, leaving her little time to get all of the windows shut and locked.

She started with Oliver's room and found that he was sound asleep as usual. A sonic boom wouldn't wake that kid. She closed and locked his window, smiling at the purple elephant night light that he kept on each and every night. It had been a gift from Nana, and he said that it kept the shadow man out of his room. That is a whole other story.

She made her way around the house, ending with the kitchen. The dishes were piled up in the sink. Oliver had friends over for lunch and they were determined to eat them out of house and home and then leave the mess behind for her to clean up, which she would gladly do. Anything to keep Oliver's home life somewhat normal since their parents decided to travel the world all summer. She had begun to wonder if they were planning on coming back.

They had taken their entire savings, deposited it into her bank account, and told her if she needed more to just send a text. Over $50,000 had been deposited into her account. That was enough money to feed them for years.

She finished up the dishes and then sat down to watch a movie. The wind was still howling outside, thunder was rolling, and the night sky lit up as the lightning flashed. After scrolling through the selection, she came across….

"The Shadow Man. Half man, half shadow. He will haunt you while you sleep and sometimes visit you while you are awake." Was this the same 'Shadow Man' Oliver spoke of? He must have watched this movie, and this was where he got that name from. It was all beginning to make sense: the night light; the mention of the 'Shadow Man'. She knew that she just had to watch the movie to see what was scaring Oliver so much.

The Shadow Man

Was she sleeping…?

Olivia sat up, rubbing her eyes, wondering what time it was. The last thing she could remember was turning on the movie, 'Shadow Man'. She must have fallen asleep within minutes. The movie was still playing, casting shadows on the walls as the lights faded in and out. The sound was oddly muted: she felt as if she were watching an old picture movie as the woman sat up, screaming at the shadowy figure hovering over her. The woman in the movie then sat up in her bed, placing a hand on either cheek, her mouth was wide open as if she were screaming; but no noise came out as a shadowy figure began to descend closer to where she sat.

Slightly creeped out, she turned the television off, and the room plunged into total darkness. Getting up from the couch and making her way to the fridge for a bottle of water, she turned on all of the lights along the way. Water bottle in hand, she made her way back to the couch. She should go back to bed, but the couch seemed to be calling her name.

Olivia laid back down on the couch, closed her eyes, and slipped off to sleep. After what seemed to be only a few minutes, Olivia's eyes opened and immediately she was plunged into utter terror to discover a dark shadowed man in a top hat standing in the corner of the living room. Olivia opened her mouth to scream, but nothing came out but air. The man in the top hat seemed to be drifting closer to her and she could do nothing but stare. She could not move; she could not scream; she could not do anything but lie there in absolute terror.

This went on for what seemed to be an hour, and then the front door to the cottage suddenly opened and Olivia finally found her breath and could speak, or at least whisper, "Who are you?"

The silhouetted man appeared to float ever closer to where she was lying on the couch.

"Your worst nightmare!" the Shadow Man's voice boomed, as all of the lights in the house turned off, plunging the house into darkness while outside the storm raged on. Olivia and Oliver were never seen or heard from, ever again.

The Staircase

***

Robert Graver

There is something in this house that I cannot escape. I can't quite explain it. What I can explain though, is that there's a reason why every eleventh sentence begins as a poem. It all begins with why houses aren't built with eleven steps anymore.

Architects can be a suspicious bunch, and my father wasn't exempt from this. Many will skip building floor thirteen, and jump straight from twelve to fourteen. When they're building houses, everything from the colour of the paint on the porch, to the type of flowers planted outside. All of these can affect the 'luck' of the homeowner. For the most part, my dad told me these quirks were more traditional than anything else. All but one.

Yesterday, upon the stair,
I met a man who wasn't there.
He wasn't there again today,
I wish, I wish he'd go away.

When I came home last night at three,
The man was waiting there for me.
But when I looked around the hall,

I couldn't see him there at all.
Go away, don't come back anymore,
Go away, don't slam the door.

Last night I saw upon the stair,
A little man who wasn't there.
He wasn't there again today,
Oh, how I wish he'd go away.

My dad told me this poem when I was first looking to buy a house. He said that a poet and educator called William Hughes Mearns wrote it many years ago. At the time it didn't really make any sense. All I remember was he used it as a warning for me to not buy somewhere that had eleven steps. My response was sarcastic as usual, something about making sure to buy a new broom to go with a new house. I knew the drill. He shook his head. He seemed far away. I only wish I had listened to him back then. If only I had listened.

I know it sounds like bullshit, son,
But trust me when I say,
Never buy a house with steps numbered eleven,
Not unless you want those steps,
To lead you straight to heaven.

You won't believe me now, I know that much is true,
So, take these words, written down,
And let them guide and show you,

When you buy that fateful home,
There is but one thing you must do.

Count the steps, if nothing else,
Do let that be your guide,
If there are eleven there,
It's best you run and hide.

Those were my father's final words. He passed away last year. I made the promise not to buy a house with eleven steps, but my mind was elsewhere. If only I'd listened, maybe then I wouldn't have to live in constant fear, always looking over my shoulder. My mind was on the girl with red hair and a gunfighter grin. She occupied all my thoughts, all my daydreams, everything. There wasn't any room left for what I thought was such a small promise to take root. So, I forgot it. God damn me, I forgot!

Dearest father, I hope this finds you well,
These endless thoughts drip from my soul,
Every single word secretly paints a fairytale,
Of when we will melt into one.

Eyes forfeit sight to the pain,
Cold scalpels steel whispers,
Tear at my very core.
As I cling to memories of you,
I am so scared, so scared.
I need you with me.

In my last words that I write for you,
Is it enough to tell you,
That in my death, there was a light,
Shining through the painful darkness.
Was it a blinding vision of your eternal smile?

These poems are becoming incoherent, and I barely remember even writing them anymore. Something has a grip around my mind and is forcing pen to paper. It has to be those stairs, those fucking stairs!

I thought the house was perfect. Large open windows drank in the morning light. The deck was old wood, solid and stained, and dotted with columns. There was an office for me and a fireplace for Daisy. Best of all, there was space, empty now, but vibrating with potential. Wherever I looked, I saw images of kids and dogs, memories just waiting for us to catch up. If only I wasn't so distracted by new beginnings.

Halfway down the stairs is a step where I like to sit,
There isn't any other stair quite like it.
I'm not at the bottom, I'm not at the top,
So, this is the step where I always stop.

I feel the breath of wind, an icy gust of air,
I feel it on my neck, a truly ghostly affair.
My skin is cold, my hair on end,
I'm all afear that death will soon be my friend.

In my distracted frame of mind, I was so keen to purchase this house, this perfect home. I didn't count the steps when the estate agent began to show us around upstairs. Not then, not until after the ink was dry on the purchase agreement, and our rented moving van was parked in the driveway.

Coming from an apartment, Daisy and I didn't have many belongings. The doctor told Daisy not to lift too much or exert herself, and I was stubborn enough to figure that I could handle it myself.

So, move in day was dragging and I was struggling to see over the nightstand I was holding, halfway up the stairs. That was when I heard heavy footfall on the steps behind me. I called out to Daisy, "I can handle the upstairs stuff," shifting to look behind me, "if you want to get started with-"

The stairs were empty behind me. I felt it then, a sense of unease, mixed with guilt, as if I'd done something wrong or forgotten something important.

"Hey babe," I called. I shouted out her name,
"What's up? Need a hand?" her gorgeous voice it came.
"No, I'm fine, just wanted to hear your voice."
"You know I'd help, but I don't really have a choice."

I moved slowly up the stairs, listening with intent.
I reached the top with laboured breath, now completely spent.
I turned around, and looked on down, the wooden flight below.

I counted them, I counted sure, I counted nice and slow.
Eleven steps, there was no doubt, of this much I was sure.
That broken promise made, of which I now had to endure.

"One, two, three, four, five, wait, shit," I said to myself. My breathing was shallow and coming out in short bursts, "I skipped one, fuck this."

I began to walk down the stairs. I carefully noted each step. As my foot touched number eleven at the bottom, the last step, I felt a brush against my neck. Almost like fingertips. I whirled around so quickly I almost fell.

"You all right?" Daisy called out from the kitchen.

"Fine," I lied, "must be new house jitters."

There were no jitters, only fear,
These stairs were such a creep.
Old and antique wood,
The stairs were far from cheap.

Banisters and balustrades,
Loomed above my head,
I had a feeling,
That I'd soon wind up dead.

The rest of the move-in went smoothly, no

hiccups or any more issues with the stairs. Every time I headed up or down them, I would go slow, and I would listen. I never noticed anything else that day, but I made sure to count each time, and the number never changed.

A week after moving in, Daisy and I were woken up by the sound of someone running up the staircase. The footsteps were so loud and startling, each one like a hammer against a board.

"Jesus, Stephen, what the fuck?" Daisy shouted, jumping out of bed.

I scrambled to the bedroom door and turned the lock, keeping my back against it.

"Call the cops," I said, listening for any sounds outside the door. "Under the bed, don't come out until I say so."

I dashed to the closet, on the far side of the room,
Fighting through the shadows of the dark bedroom gloom.
My fingers fumbled and slipped as I tried to enter the code,
My hands were shaking and my fright it surely showed.
Finally, in my lockbox safe inside,
A Smith and Wesson gun in there did hide.

I pulled it out, and climbed under the bed,
To lie in wait for that thing that wished me dead.
Eight long minutes passed, as we sat there in fear,
The blue lights shone and the sirens we could hear.

As I heard the police cars pull up, I crept out from underneath the bed, my hands still shaking. I ushered for Daisy to stay put, at least until the cops had given us the all clear. I put the gun away and crept down the stairs. On the last step, I felt something yank my hair. When I turned around, there was nothing there, nothing behind me. Only an empty stairwell, bathed in the landing light. I could nearly taste my own pulse, a greasy, panicked thing. The police knocked, hard. I backed away, never taking my eyes from the stairs until the front door was open. The cops didn't find anything – no signs of an intruder or forced entry – and left us to spend the rest of the sleepless night downstairs.

That staircase looked so boring, bathed in the morning light,
That damned staircase that had given us such a fright.
I was worried that my wife would brush off my idea,
We must leave, and with haste, of which I had made clear.

"Let's give the place another chance," the words I thought she'd say,
"I think you're right, let's go now, waste not another day."
A protective hand stroked against her bump, now big and round.
"I love you," came my words, before that awful sound,
The stairs did creak, and wife did shriek
And my head began to pound.

The rest of the day consisted of very loud phone calls with estate agents, and some quiet moments where Daisy and I just sat on the couch, looking at the house we were giving up. It didn't bother me as much as I thought it would. I knew, looking at Daisy as she began packing, that she carried my home with her wherever she went.

"I'm gonna go talk to those fuckers in person," I said. "Those estate agent creeps are hiding something, I'm sure of it."

Daisy was lying on the couch, her sleepless night clearly catching up. I glanced over at the stairs.

"Daisy, if you need to rest, that's fine, but please, just promise me that you'll stay downstairs, okay?"

She opened one green eye, giving me the shadow of a grin.

"Don't worry, cowboy, even wild horses couldn't take me back up there."

I argued loud, I argued clear, these creeps were gonna pay,
I said it loud, I said it clear, everything I had to say.
The house we bought, there's something odd,
Something you're not telling us, say it now or so help me God.

The house it seems or as it turns out, has a troubled past,
No gruesome murders or satanic rituals had been cast.
But a string of awful accidents left a grizzly trail,
As I heard, it hit me hard, my face turned ghostly pale.

My mouth was dry from my raising voice,
I had to leave; I knew I had no choice.
I called my wife, no answer from her phone,
She's just asleep, I told myself, as I raced on home,

If something was wrong, my Daisy was a fighter,
The dread swelled in my stomach as I drove,
Like a cancer pulling tighter.

I found Daisy dead at the foot of the stairs. She was twisted and bent like a doll dropped on the floor. Thick violet bruises covered her body. I held her for several minutes before calling for help. She was clearly gone. As I waited for the ambulance to arrive, I heard the slow creak of footsteps moving down the stairs towards me, creeping closer until they were just inches away. I couldn't see a thing, just empty, bloodstained stairs.

My morning was well documented: the confrontation with the estate agents meant that I couldn't have been home with Daisy at the time of her death. I overheard the cops talking to the medical examiner, and saying that she had been dragged up the stairs before falling down or being thrown.

Make it stop, make this pounding in my head stop.
Fill my lungs with air, give me one more day,
Make his dreams come true.
He understands right?
That I'm not coming back.

I don't know what happened.
Who would've thought,
That my life would end up like this.
I never got the chance to see his face,

To touch his hair, and now, it's too late.

I didn't mean to hurt him, not like this,
I can't feel my legs, and I can't even cry.
How could someone die like this.

I never knew that silence could cut so deep,
Or that you could twist the blade.
Now I curse all of your beautiful lies,
I love you and goodbye.

These are the last words that I write for you,
Are they enough to tell you,
That in my death the light that shone,
Shone through my painful darkness,
Was a blinding vision of your eternal smile.

Cold scalpels steel whispers,
Tear at my very core,
As I cling to my memories of you.

I wasn't arrested, but was told not to leave town whilst an investigation was carried out. The note my wife had written as she died was cryptic and confusing. I took the bloodstained piece of paper I pried from her cold hands, and hid it from the medics. I was told to stay at home. I can hear it pacing the stairs as I write this down. Sometimes it takes soft, deliberate steps, the wood groaning under its heavy, unseen weight. Other times, it runs; it wants me to hear it. Now and then, it mimics the thuds of something, or someone falling down the stairs. Daisy. I'm so sorry.

Last night I forgot,
How the sound of your voice whispered,
Sweet goodbyes.

Your eyes, left to die,
I'm alone to understand why.
Why not one more night?
One last kiss goodbye?

My sweet love tonight,
I hope the stars spell out your name.
Where you are, kiss my closing eyes,
Help me sleep.

Without you I'm so lost,
Tonight, I cry.
Tell me why.

I close my eyes and you are all I see,
Goodbye,
Goodbye to you my love,
I won't forget you,
I'll see you soon.

I finished what would be my final poem. My final verse of this twisted tale.

I poured the gasoline around the bedroom, the hallways, the couch. I poured it everywhere. The last place I made sure was covered the most...the stairs. Those *fucking* stairs. I can still smell it now. It reminds me of summertime, of fresh cut grass and of a girl with red hair and a-

I'm going to burn this house down and then I don't know what I'll do. But at least there will be one fewer staircase with eleven steps. The next time you find yourself climbing up to the bedroom, or down to the basement, do yourself a favour. Count.

Oh, look at you, you miserable fool,
Get off our knees,
Your prayers fall upon deaf ears.
God's turned his back on you.

Heavens gates are shut,
And now, you're knocking on the Devil's door.
I've been expecting you for some time, sir.
Allow me to introduce myself.

I'm the one who pulls on all the strings, son.
You're lucky I don't kill you where you stand.

I heard the words so clearly as the house crumbled around me. There could only be one explanation for my craziness, for my obedience. I had been following a set of rules my own mind had set out. That number, eleven. It haunted me for years after Daisy died, and I've slowly gone insane. There can't be any devil or monster haunting me. It has to be all in my head...right? Please tell me I'm right? I don't know how I survived the fire. I am writing this from an asylum somewhere atop a hill, but the entrance has eleven steps, and I don't think I can ever leave.

Monster

***

Robert Graver

Addiction — noun — the fact or condition of being addicted to a particular substance or activity.

Addiction is a psychological and physical inability to stop consuming a chemical, drug, activity, or substance, even though it is causing psychological and physical harm. Every year, addiction to alcohol, tobacco, illicit drugs, and prescription opioids costs the U.S. economy upward of $740 billion. It cost me my mother.

It took her slowly. It took her on a ride, to the far end of the abyss, to the other side and back again. It sang her to sleep, pulling her deep into the impression of the mattress I found her on so often.

I was eight when her teeth began to fall out. She left them on the side of the bathtub, forgetting, or even not knowing that she'd lost them. I kept them safe, so she wouldn't be broken forever. I placed the lost pieces of my mum in an empty pill bottle, hoping to one day be able to fix her, return her missing parts. Make her whole again.

Our house wasn't great, it was old, rotting from the inside and cold. Always so cold. The whole place fell into disrepair: the wallpaper peeling, carpets fraying, the radiators bled dry and cried rust in the winter. I'm pretty sure we had more rodents living in the crawl space beneath our house than the subway system in New York. But none of that mattered. It was still our house, and Janey made it a home.

My sister, Janey, mothered me, gave me the love that we both yearned for. She kissed my scrapes and bruises, sticking the cartoon plasters on my knees. She would brush my tangled and matted hair before school every day, never batting an eyelid when I screamed and smacked her if she caught a tangle.

She would pack my lunch box, cutting the crusts from my sandwich and making sure the squares were all equal. It was the little things. She always put me before herself.

She would let me have the hot water in the shower, sacrificing the heat, so I would be clean and warm, leaving herself nothing but cold water. All for me.

Janey had dark hair, like Mum. I had blonde hair, like Dad, not that I knew who he was. I had only been told by Mum that my hair was similar to his. Maybe that's what turned her against me? Always made her closer to Janey. She reminded her less of the coward that left her alone, two children to care for and no income. What a piece of shit.

I'd give anything to have Janey run her fingers through my hair again. I'd even welcome the pain when she tugs on a knot. She moved out when she turned eighteen. The pain of her leaving still hasn't healed.

Keeping track of Mum's moods was difficult. It was as though she was a different person, dependent on the crutch, relying on copious amounts of alcohol to get her through each day.

If she drank just a little, she seemed perfect, the best mum in the world. I could forgive being woken up at two in the morning, because she would have pancakes dripping with maple syrup, or waffles and ice cream. Sometimes, if she had woken up from a heavy night, too hungover to drink more, she would phone up our reception at school and say both myself and Janey were sick. We'd take a drive to the seaside and play all day on the beach and in the amusement arcades.

If she drank heavily, she would be out all night. Sometimes she would bring home random men, filling the kitchen with cigarette smoke and empty beer cans. Janey and I would try and sleep through it, our covers pulled up high, smothering our heads with our pillows, just to try and drown out the shouting and music that blared relentlessly throughout the night.

We would go downstairs in the morning, greeted by strangers, asking us where the coffee or tea was kept, our mum nowhere to be seen. Some nights she wouldn't even come home, she would be gone for days at a time, but always left the fridge stocked and a note on the table saying she loved us.

If mum didn't drink enough, she would break. She couldn't function, the simplest of tasks seemed too much for her to handle. The fridge would remain empty, the bins overflowing, the whole house a state.

She would chain-smoke cigarette after cigarette, filling the whole place with a grey haze. Mum would snap at the smallest things. I remember spilling my cereal one morning on the sofa cushions, and she lost it completely.

I was dragged off by my legs, left on the floor in shock. Mum grabbed the cushions and took them to the garden before going to town on them with the grass trimmer, shredding them to pieces like an overactive puppy with its favourite toy. All Janey and I could do was sit and watch, cuddled together on the bare sofa, the springs digging into our backs.

Mum was the worst when she drank *too* much. She would break down and cry at anything and everything. The toast landing the wrong way on the floor, sent her into floods of tears. The stupid plastic seal on the milk bottle, not tearing off properly, started with fits of laughter and soon descended into the full waterworks.

Janey was never herself when Mum was like this. She would retreat into herself, somewhere in her mind where she couldn't the feel hurt or pain of seeing Mum this way. She would stay up all night watching old movies, reciting the words by heart. I would wake up to find mother covered in vomit, passed out in her bed, wet from pissing herself. I cried and cried, scared she wouldn't wake up. Janey would reassure me that she was just sleeping heavily, like a princess in my story books she read to me at night. Janey has taken on the role of Mum to me.

It was late August and Mum had been gone for two days. I had just turned thirteen, Janey seventeen. Mum called from a payphone, neither of us knew where she was calling from, but we both secretly wished she would stay there.

She asked how my birthday was, which was yesterday. I didn't even get to see her on my first day as a teenager. Janey had bought me a few small presents: some lip gloss and glitter based make up, not expensive items, but I didn't question where she got the money from. I didn't care. All I cared about was spending the day with her, and that she actually remembered my birthday.

The day itself was great. We had taken the bus to the beach and watched the waves crash, and stayed late until the sun began to set over the horizon, painting red and orange hues in the sky. We took the last bus home and I sat down to watch evening cartoons.

It all started to go downhill from that night. There was tension and anger in the air. It began when Janey stumbled and tripped down the bottom step of the stairs. I helped her up but she just kept falling backwards. When I finally managed to pull her up completely, I felt her warm breath on my cheek, tinged with the woody scent of cheap bourbon. She fell back again. I couldn't let her stay down. I knew she wouldn't get back up, just like Mum.

I stared down at the pathetic, glazed expression on her face, her black hair stuck to her lips, and all I could see was our Mum. That was the last straw, I had snapped.

I ran through the hallway, slamming the kitchen door behind me. I grabbed every bottle of booze I could reach and tipped them down the sink. Janey crashed through the kitchen door, sending it flying into the wall, the handle embedding itself into the plaster. Another hole in the house that couldn't be fixed.

She came at me, and tried to snatch the last bottle as I was pouring it down the sink. The sickly smell I had become accustomed to clung inside my nostrils, like it clung to my mother's breath.

Janey clipped the neck of the bottle, sending it flying to the floor between us, smashing into thousands of tiny shards. The pieces glistened, like stars that had be pulled from the sky, pieces we would never be able to put back together. I began to cry, watching as Janey knelt to the floor, picking up the broken mess, always trying to fix things, even when it was too late. I stormed off to my bedroom, not able to stand seeing her in this state.

I must have dozed off; the smell of onions and garlic woke me up. I could hear pots and pans clinking in the kitchen, the faint hum of the stove, and Janey singing along to a 'My Chemical Romance' song.

She always listened to them when she was upset. Their depressing lyrics, dark tonal guitars and the minor scales used in the piano tracks always seemed to perk Janey up, pull her back from the dark place she was in. As I cracked open the door an inch, I could hear the lyrics a lot clearer:

You're never coming home, never coming home.
And all the things that you never ever told me.
And all the smiles that are ever gonna haunt me.
Never coming home, never coming home.
Could I? Should I?

I didn't understand how they fit into the song she was listening too, but they seemed to resonate somewhere in my mind with the situation we were in. Perhaps that's the power music has on people. They relate to lyrics, even if they aren't anything to do with what the artist is singing about, but the words, the melody, the tune — everything about a song, impacts differently upon each person who listens.

I pulled the door open fully and descended the stairs, the aroma wafting my way from the kitchen made my mouth water. It was a real smell. A proper scent. Not the plastic shit that comes from microwave meals I had become accustomed to.

Janey knew my favourite food was Spaghetti Bolognese. For as long as I could remember, it was always *the* best comfort food. I wandered into the kitchen, watching as Janey shook her hips to the music and stirred away at the sauce on top of the stove.

The table was laid, something Mum never stayed sober enough to do, let alone remember my favourite meal, or birthday for that fact. Food was served, and with every bite I forgave Janey for what happened earlier. I couldn't be mad at her.

After we had eaten, our bellies full, we took turns washing the dishes. Something clean in the house; probably the only thing clean in the house.

The kitchen window began steaming up, another trigger that Mum would flip her shit over. Something about the condensation, or the water dripping drove her crazy. In an almost instinctive action, I opened the window, allowing the steam to dissipate out into the night air. We both stopped washing up and looked into each other's eyes. We had both heard the cry coming from the end of the garden. It was more than likely the baby crying in the Johnson's house, or Marlboro the cat.

Janey had a knack for naming anything and everything. Usually ironic, or clearly unusual names for whatever it was that needed one.

The first time we saw Marlboro, we were sat on the grass in the garden, it curled around my ankles, its tail standing on end. There was no collar, so Janey took a glance around, spotting a pile of empty cigarette packets, overflowing from the garden bin. Marlboro Reds, hence, the cats name.

We both saw a lot more of the cat after that. It was skinny and tatty and liked to hang out in the alley near our house; junky alley, as Janey called it. The local hotspot for shooting up or wasting away.

I remember when I wanted to feed Marlboro, but Janey stopped me.

"You can't give it anything, it will just come back wanting more."

Thinking back on the memory, I don't think she was talking about the cat.

We finished drying the dishes and sat outside on the garden step, staring up at the stars, flickering brightly in the summer night sky. Janey pointed at a constellation, her naming process and storytelling as unusual as ever.

"That one over there, see it? That's Jonnie Walker. It first appeared after the angels had a wild party and left bottles of whiskey all over the place."

I giggled at her stupid game, but I loved it.

"And see that one above the roof over there?" she said, pointing towards the sky, "That one's called The Ashtray, left behind by the angels on a smoke break."

Janey let out a sigh. I cuddled up to her, lending her my warmth.

"They say, if you wish upon a star, all your wishes will come true, right Janey?" I looked up my sister, waiting for her reply.

"They do. Let's wish Jo."

So, we wished. We wished long and hard, until our thoughts were interrupted by the cry again. It sounded closer now. Maybe because we were sat in the garden, but it was definitely human, baby like, lost and all on its own.

"It has to be the baby from that house." I said, climbing to my feet. "I should go and check, do you want to call for the Johnsons and see if everything is okay?" Janey didn't reply. I sighed, stepped onto the grass and muttered under my breath, "Guess I'll do everything myself then."

I was no more than a few feet away from the steps when Janey shouted at me.

"Jo!"

I looked back, her hand was on the door handle, and she was ushering me inside. The smile on my face quickly faded when I saw the expression on hers.

"Get inside. Now!"

I turned around, seeing what she had. In the shrubs at the back of the garden was a person, crouched on the floor, their knees tucked up against their chest with their arms wrapped around them. They were swaying back and forth, like someone in shock, or the characters you see on telly in the nuthouse wearing straitjackets.

The same crying sound was coming from this person's mouth, but it was clearer now. It wasn't a baby. This person was mimicking the sound, almost perfectly. Without warning, they snapped upright, the darkness obscuring their face. They were tall and thin, too thin though, too thin to be a normal person.

Panic set in. I turned and ran inside, Janey not far behind me. Even now, she had waited until I was inside before slamming the door shut and locking it, her fingers fumbling at the catches.

She was still mothering me, making sure I was safe, before herself. She grabbed my hand and pulled my head towards her chest, forcing me down so I couldn't see into the garden.

"Jo, I'm going to call the police. Everything is going to be—" She stopped. A stark realisation. "My phones on the steps outside."

I began to think how I could help, if I could. My phone, as old and second hand as it was, still worked, and it was upstairs in my bedroom. A gentle tapping filled the silence of the kitchen. Both of us sat on the floor, fingers interlocked, gripping so tightly it hurt.

I tried to sneak a look at whoever was tapping on the window, quickly met by a forceful hand on the back of my head from Janey, keeping me from seeing.

Whoever was outside had begun to hit the window harder. They weren't using their hands or fists though; they were smacking their head against the glass. Each hit harder and faster, the pane of glass surely about to break.

Silence. Just as I was about to ask if I could look yet, the glass shattered. I screamed, bolting away from Janey and bounding up the stairs. Janey was on my heels, still blocking my view of whomever it was.

We hurried into the bathroom and turned the knob, the only room upstairs with a working lock. We sat and huddled together, listening to the same mock cry as before. A baby looking for its mother, an animal trapped in a snare, calling for help.

I sat with my back against the door, feet firmly planted on the bottom of the toilet bowl. Janey made sure I didn't move while she looked around the room for something sharp. She managed to find a pair of scissors in the cupboard and joined me on the floor, her feet against the toilet as well.

The crying had begun to sound more like laughter. A mocking, shrill giggle, rising in volume before abruptly stopping and repeating again. I heard one of the bedroom doors slam open. It was my room, the tell-tale creaking of the hinges. They were looking for us.

"What do we do?" I whispered.

The next door slammed open. Mum's room. Janey stood up, handing me the scissors. I pushed them back towards her, refusing to take them. I didn't want to think about what would happen if I

49

had to try and use them. She pushed them back, harder this time.

Something crashed into the wall separating the bathroom and the room next door. The next doorway along the landing that this person would reach was the bathroom, we had no time to squabble over some scissors.

Another crash came from Mum's room. Were they searching for us? Or searching for something? I took the scissors.

"I'm going to go and get your phone." Janey looked adamant, despite my shaking head and tear-filled eyes. I opened my mouth to speak, but she quickly put her hand over it, keeping me silent.

"It's the only way I can call the police, and then everything will be fine. I promise."

I continued to shake my head, tears streaming down my face now.

"When I go, you need to lock the door behind me as quickly as you can, okay? Don't open it for anyone or anything, not even me. Just stay in here until it's safe. Promise me."

I carried on shaking my head as Janey lifted her hand from my mouth, reaching towards the lock. She mouthed the words '*promise*' as she silently unlocked the door and slid out into the darkness of the hallway.

I stood with the door open for a moment, enough to see her figure disappear before slamming it shut and locking it again. As soon as the lock clicked into place, the handle began to rattle. Rising up and down so violently it knocked loose a screw, rolling onto the floor and into the beam of moonlight coming in through the window. The rattling stopped.

Silence.

I sat with my back against the door again, trembling and crying, my hands gripping the scissors tightly. The sound of my heavy breathing filled the room. I cast my mind to all the monsters that Janey read about in stories, and how I wished they were real sometimes. In this moment, I took that all back. I wished they would just go away.

"Jo?" came a voice from the other side of the door. I jumped, almost dropping the scissors. "What's going on, baby?"

"Mum?" My voice cracked, strained from crying, "Is that you?"

I took back everything I thought earlier. Not wanting her to come back, wishing she would stay gone.

"Everything is fine, sweetie. Just let me in, please."

I shuffled away from the door slightly, the handle moving up and down more slowly this time.

"Please, baby. I'm sorry. I'm so sorry I missed your birthday. I'm sorry that I'm such a terrible mum." Her voice broke, "Please just let me in, baby."

I moved back against the door, squeezing my eyes shut tightly, wishing for everything to stop and go away, pretending it was all a dream and I would wake up soon.

I began to stand up, ready to let her in. She sounded so hurt and sorry. I just wanted to give her a hug and forgive her for forgetting.

"That's right Josephine, everything is fine, just let us in." Janey's voice came through the door, full of warmth and soft-spoken as usual.

I pulled my hand away from the lock. Janey never called me by my full name. A pounding fist started hitting the door. The handle rattling again.

"Let us in!" Janey's voice was no longer gentle. It had a deep, demonic sound to it, followed by the same high-pitched laughter and giggles from before.

"Let us in. Let us in. Let us in."

The pounding continued. The chanting continued. I held my hands to my ears, trying to block out the noise.

"You're not Janey! And you're not my Mum! Go away!" I yelled, as loud as I could, making sure they could hear me over the pounding and their chants. That voice that wasn't Janey. It wasn't the same voice that yelled at me when I wouldn't give her stuff back, or sung to me when I was sad. It wasn't her voice.

I heard banging and shouting from downstairs. The pounding on the door had stopped. I heard footsteps rushing up the stairs, a gunshot, and a loud thud. I shut my eyes and screamed. I didn't open them again until I heard the bathroom door get kicked in.

When I looked around, there was no demon or monster, Janey, or Mum, just a police officer standing in the doorway. He scooped me up and carried me downstairs. I peered through tear filled eyes at my mum's bedroom as we went past.

Pillows and sheets were everywhere, torn apart like a fox to a chicken. Drawers pulled out from their resting spots, strewn across the floor.

As the officer carried me outside, I saw Janey sitting in the back of an ambulance, her face lit up by the flashing lights. She smiled at me. *That* was Janey.

We sat in silence as various paramedics and police officers entered the house and exited again. I sat and cried in the back of the ambulance, under the stars with made up constellation names until they came out of the house with a stretcher on wheels, the death trolley. There was a body underneath, covered by the black bag disguising who it was. But I knew then, in that moment, it was Mum.

There had been no demon or monsters. No bad person trying to break into our house. It was just Mum, on a week-long bender, drunk and high on whatever she could get her hands on. Something had finally snapped in her head, and this time, Janey couldn't fix it. No matter how much she tried, Mum was too broken to fix.

Janey had seen her in the garden, the tall, thin figure. That was why she didn't want me to see. To see the track marks all over her arms, vomit and blood staining her face and clothes. The deranged look in her eyes, desperate for just one more fix.

Mum had searched the kitchen for any booze, all of which I had tipped away earlier that day. With no luck in the kitchen, she stripped her room, searching for any sort of stash. That was when she made her way to the bathroom, wanting her secret supply, hidden in the cistern, just on the other side of the locked door. She was so high and drunk that she could somehow mimic Janey's voice, perfectly.

It turns out that addiction is the *real* monster. Out to eat you alive, slowly, from the inside out. The kind of monster that hides in a bottle of whiskey, or in the end of a needle. At the end of a long list of reasons not to get up in the morning.

Sometimes, the monster has been in front of you the whole time.

Part Two: Murders and Mysteries

Who Dun It?

Welcome to our mystery section,
A place of lies and misdirection,
An island resort full of woe,
A quiet town, and Sheriff Joe,

Follow the tunnel, where does it lead?
Who's the killer? Who did the deed?
Many questions that must be asked,
But now the skies are overcast.

Hang in the web, that has been spun,
Spousal ties have come undone,
There's evidence here we must destroy,
Turn the page, disengage, and enjoy.

- R. Graver

Hélène's Adventure

***

Anne-Charlotte Gerbaud

Part One: The White Pearl Necklace

The sun had not risen yet, the street was extremely quiet, the snow was covering all the city like a white blanket and the temperature was announcing a rude winter on the 29th of November 1865 when Hélène, a young maid from Brittany who had been working with the Baudel de Vaudrecourt's family for her entire life, like her mother and her grandmother before her, woke up after hearing someone knocking violently on the door of the tiny room she was living in with another maid on the last floor of the private mansion located at 17 Place des Vosges in Paris.

The clamour was confusing and scary and Hélène looked at the other maid, who was wide awake and as surprised as her, stood up quickly, put on her light blue dressing gown to protect herself from the cold, and walked towards the door which she did not need to open as the butler was now entering in the company of the scullery maid, the laundry maid, the housekeeper, the chauffeur, the cook, the first footman and, most importantly and surprisingly, Monsieur and Madame Baudel de Vaudrecourt, who both looked displeased to be in the attic of their private mansion as they chimed in unison: "Hélène, where is Madame's white pearl necklace?"

The room was almost too tiny for the crowd gathered here, shouting, staring, and pointing fingers at Hélène who was trying to figure out what was happening and why she was accused of having stolen the white pearl necklace that Napoleon III himself had offered to Madame Baudel de Vaudrecourt the last time the couple was invited at a reception held at the Tuilerie Palace and which Madame loved to show off by wearing her light green silk dress, with a wide and off-the-shoulder neckline, each time a reception was organised at the mansion, that is to say, every Tuesday and Saturday.

Hélène claimed she was innocent but the hostile crowd, led by Madame, did not believe her and were all looking for the necklace in Hélène's personal belongings, which were stored in the small, old wardrobe on the left-hand side of the room when you entered, when a cry from Caroline, the other maid sleeping in the same room as Hélène, froze everyone as she cried, "Hélène is innocent: I was told to hide the necklace here but I hid it in the silver vase in the dining room," she said while Madame was blushing with rage and shame, stunned by the fact that Caroline was revealing the truth.

Hélène was shocked, but instead of blaming Caroline, because she knew the poor thing had no other choice but to follow Madame's order, she held her in her arms and told her she forgave her before looking at Madame and Monsieur de Baudel de Vaudrecourt and the rest of the crowd gathered there to say: "Madame, I know you do not like me because you feel somewhat jealous and you are afraid that your husband wants me to join him in his bed, which, I am not going to lie, he has already asked a few times; but this is the last straw that breaks the camel's back and I am going to resign and leave you and those white pearls that I despise forever."

Part Two: A Mysterious Encounter

This is how Hélène left the Baudel de Vaudrecourt's house. We were on the 29th of November 1865, and she was now a jobless and homeless woman. She was wandering in Paris when she heard cries from a backstreet nearby. She followed the sound and walked in a cul-de-sac. A strange mist was all around her, and she realised that she was alone. Her heart was beating fast.

"Please stay, Hélène. don't be scared," a male voice said.

Hélène stopped, "Who's there?"

"Edmond Poincaré, and you are Hélène Guégen."

"How do you know my name? And what do you want from me?"

"I'm not going to harm you, Hélène. I know you've just lost your job and I was wondering if you wanted to work with me."

"How do you…"

"I know it must be very confusing. But let me explain. I'm looking for a novice to whom I could hand over my task of protecting the world against beasts from the underworld."

Hélène couldn't believe what she had just heard. This man had probably escaped from an asylum.

"I've never been in an asylum," the man replied as if he had read Hélène's mind. "Let me show you something and, after that, if you're not convinced, you can just go to Judith's brothel as you planned."

Hélène's eyes widened. She stayed silent for a while and finally said: "I'll come only if you promise that you won't hurt me… or kill me."

Edmond came closer and removed his hat.

"I cannot promise you won't be hurt," he said, "but I can promise that I'll do everything to protect you. Would you mind taking my hand?"

Hélène took his hand with hesitation. At the moment her fingers met his palm, she felt she was thrown somewhere at a very high speed. The whirlwind finally stopped and Hélène felt very nauseous, although she didn't fall on the ground.

Edmond placed his hat back on his head. He smiled at Hélène.

"That was very well done for a first time. You'll get used to it, trust me."

Hélène wasn't sure what he meant by "a first time". Did he expect her to come with him again? How could he be so sure of it?

She quickly turned her head. They were in the Père Lachaise cemetery and someone was weeping behind a mausoleum.

"Follow me, but be quiet," Edmond whispered.

As they got closer to the mausoleum, two eyes shone in the dark. It was a little girl.

"Will you help me?" she said sobbing.

"Show me your true nature, vampire!" Edmond pulled out a dagger from his waistcoat.

The little girl let out a piercing cry. Her mouth was wide open, but it had a weird angle as if her jaw was dislocated. Long sharp teeth were growing rapidly.

She tried to jump on Hélène, but the old man was faster and stabbed the beast in the heart. It instantly turned into ashes.

"What was that?" Hélène was panting.

"A vampire. They fool their victims to drink their blood."

"But how can I help you fight those monsters? I'm just a maid!"

"You have the mark. Am I wrong if I tell you that you have moles on your shoulder that looked like Orion's constellation? The constellation looks like that." He started to draw the stars on the ground.

Hélène put her hand on her shoulder. He was right.

"What do you want from me?" she asked.

"I want you to become my novice."

"What if I refuse?"

"You're free to decide. But let me invite you into my house. If you're not convinced in seven days, I'll leave you alone."

Hélène hesitated. Edmond was crazy but he seemed nice. And she didn't really want to go to her friend's brothel.

"Fine. I'm following you," she replied.

Lockdown Lodge

***

Samia Nicolas

'No one touch the body! This is a crime scene now!' Jerry asserted his authority, slipping into his day job as a homicide detective like it was a snug sleeping bag. As such, the other holiday makers who had come running in response to the screams from the Wilson's Lodge froze in place or took a step back, looking to Jerry for the next instruction; they were all glad someone seemed to know what he was doing.

'Davina, my dear. I know this is hard… but have you touched the … have you touched Adeyo?'

Davina Wilson, the victim's wife, was being held in a supportive embrace by Maggie Jorgenson. She wasn't crying yet; she was still in shock.

'No… no I just found him and … and … I c-c-…' She suddenly turned her face into Maggie's curly, candy floss hair and sobbed. She pulled out some tissue from her pocket. Jerry saw it was a piece torn from toilet paper, and maybe it was because he was jaded from the job, but his first thoughts were how wasteful it was to use it while they were trapped on this island with limited supplies.

Jerry peered around at the crowd, his trained eye already making little observations and placing them neatly in the back of his mind to turn over for a while. Mostly people were quiet. Jerry watched their eyes; one thing he knew to look for was that the person who murdered Adeyo might not want to see his dead body so soon after the kill. Jerry scanned each face while also doing a count.

'Who's not here?' he asked so suddenly that it made Phillippe Jercaux flinch and Tilly Smith gasp.

Tilly straightened her glasses and gripped her husband David's arm more tightly, as if to make sure he was still there.

'It's Tom. He's not here.' Jerry was already asking while everyone else was looking at each other in bewilderment. 'Maggie? You know where he is?'

Maggie, still gripping Davina with her own eyes red-rimmed, blinked a few times. She looked immediately guilty, as if there was a huge arrow in lights floating above her head pointing at her as Jerry scrutinised her.

'Tom went to have a smoke on the other side of the island. He always does this time of night.'

'Bit far to go just for a smoke.' Levi, the oldest and probably most self-important man there, crossed his arms. It had been obvious that he disliked Tom since the start of what had been the holiday, and he acted as if no one else liked him either.

'It's a big expensive cigar – I hate the smell of them. He smokes it far away from me and I guess it's so he can enjoy it in peace and quiet,' Maggie murmured.

Jerry felt like he was losing the room. 'Okay, listen up. I need everyone to go back to their lodges, get some sleep, and we'll all meet in the morning.'

'Get some sleep? Are you kidding me?' Levi said. Phillipe held his shoulder and shook his head – something he had to do a lot where Levi was concerned.

'What about ... Adeyo?' Tilly asked.

'I'll deal with the b- with Adeyo,' Jerry gave a smile he normally reserved for 'concerned citizens' who would give their two cents on every case he ever worked.

'Well... would you like some help? I mean, I've done a lot of reading about real crime scenes. A lot,' Tilly said to everyone's surprise.

Jerry scowled inwardly, but kept the smile on his face. Just what he needed, he thought. Amateurs.

'She has,' piped up her husband. 'I can help too.'

'Davina can come stay with me,' Maggie said, bringing the quietly sobbing woman towards the door.

As the rest of them left, Levi glared at Jerry, spurring another hand on the shoulder from Phillipe.

'At least he'll have witnesses,' Levi growled to a questioning look from his partner as they walked to their lodge just next door. Their voices carried on the still night air.

'You don't trust him?'

'Not since the day I laid eyes on him.'

'But he's a cop.'

'Exactly.'

In Wilson's Lodge, Jerry took a closer look at the body. The victim was face down, arms and legs in the classic relaxed fallen position of one limb up, one down. caused by oppositional force from dropping. That meant he was dead or unconscious before he hit the ground. Probably dead, considering the hole that went right through his torso.

'What shall we do?' Tilly asked, more nervous now that everyone had gone. Adeyo's body seemed to fill the whole lodge.

'Find a bedsheet or something. We'll cover the body, then probably use it to wrap him up. Uh, I should take photos before we do anything though. For the authorities. Once they get here.'

'Have you called them already?'

The woman's stupidity was only matched by the dimness of her husband, but Jerry was used to dealing with people like them.

'No, I came straight here when Davina screamed. Don't step in that blood, for God's sake!'

David froze and looked where he had been about to tread. The blood reached from the living room area all the way to the threshold of the bedroom. He grimaced.

Giving David a pointed glare, Jerry continued. 'I'll call them in the morning. But after they've taken pictures, we can move the body and we'll...

uh… put him on the bed. Yeah. I don't think anyone's going to be staying here anymore.'

The next morning Jerry called everyone to the clubhouse after breakfast and asked them to wait there until he joined them, which wasn't until well past 1 pm. They sat in the communal lounge and Jerry took a clearing in the centre.

'So, it's going to be a while before any police can get here. There's a storm brewing that's going to hit us later today and it may last till the end of the week, and they don't want to send anyone out. That also has implications for our supplies. How are we doing on food, Phillippe?'

'Our last delivery was enough to keep us going for about 2 weeks – I'm using the big freezers to store the meat. We'll have to start using the dried milk again soon, though, if another delivery doesn't come soon.'

There was a collective sigh from the crowd, apart from Davina, who sat as still as a gravestone.

'Well, until this pandemic is over, and we can get off this island and back to our homes, that's the deal. What about… toilet paper?' Jerry eyed everyone again at this question to gauge their response because he knew the answer already. Lack of toilet paper was about as bad as lack of food and drink.

'We'll still have to ration. The man on the delivery boat said it's a supply issue – and it's a problem all over the world,' Phillippe said.

'Well that leaves us with our third problem, Ladies and Gents. We have a murderer among us.'

Again, he watched for reactions; but since his statement wasn't exactly that shocking, he let the lack of response slide. 'So, I've brought you all here to figure out who did it.' There. That worked a little better.

'Do we know what killed him?' Tom, the man who was absent the night before, spoke. 'What could have done that to him?'

'So far, I've only done a short search of the lodge and surroundings, and I've not found anything that could have caused his injuries yet. But we have to consider that we're on a small island surrounded by the Pacific. So, the chances of us finding it are pretty slim, unless the killer is a complete idiot.' Jerry glanced at David, who looked nervously away.

'While you were all here waiting in the clubhouse, I took the liberty of searching all your lodges.'

'How dare you!' Levi stood up, only to be gently pushed back down by Phillippe. Jerry regarded him coolly.

'In my search, I found a few things that I think need to be brought to light. Don't you agree, Maggie?'

He turned to her upon calling her name, and all eyes followed his gaze. The effect was instant. She immediately broke down. Tom went to hold her, but to his shock, she pushed him away. She stood up and made to leave, but stopped short of passing the sofa she had been sitting on, her shoulders shaking, and her head bent into her hands.

'What's this all about?' Tom cried. 'What do you mean, Jerry?'

'Maggie was having an affair with Adeyo.'

The shock was felt through the room, but most profound was the effect on Davina. She suddenly came alive and screamed, then leaped from her chair in rage and ran the few steps between her chair and Maggie; but Tom stood up and caught her, holding her back while David and Levi came to assist.

'So, we have three suspects,' Jerry continued once Davina had been subdued. She now sat between Levi and Phillippe; their arms locked around hers. 'Davina, wife – who found out about the affair and took it badly. Tom, the other husband involved who found out and had his pride wounded.'

Tom's face grew dark, but he stayed silent, interesting reaction, thought Jerry.

'And finally, Maggie herself – maybe Adeyo wanted to end it; maybe he wasn't going to end it with Davina.'

Maggie sank to the floor next to the sofa. 'Never,' she whispered desperately.

'Well, it couldn't have been Tom,' Tilly said. 'He was out smoking his cigar. It didn't look like Adeyo was long passed away.'

'I put his time of death between 9 and 11 pm yesterday. When was the last time anyone saw him alive?'

'Me,' Davina said. 'We were getting ready for bed around 10:30, but I had forgotten to get our ration of water, so I went to Phillippe to get it.'

Phillippe nodded the truth of it.

'And when you got back, you claim he was already dead?'

'I don't claim anything: it's the truth!'

'The scream happened at 10:46. I know because I looked at my phone just when we heard it. Habit, I guess,' Tilly said.

'Well, that narrows down the time of death,' Jerry conceded. This was going to be harder to figure out than he thought. He had to pull out the evidence now.

'Tom, Maggie said you went to the other side of the island to smoke your cigar. But you didn't, did you? You were back in your lodge by 11:30 because I saw you with my own eyes. But you weren't walking from the north, where Maggie meant. You were walking from the south, from behind Adeyo's lodge.'

There was a satisfying number of gasps from the room.

'Yeah, so what? So, I went somewhere else to smoke it.'

'But what took so long? The south side of the dwelling area is only a few yards from the beach. You would have been back long before 11:30 had you started smoking it before Adeyo was discovered.'

'Well, I was... I was just thinking, you know? Taking in the view!'

'The view we've all grown pretty sick of, I think you'll all agree, considering we've been trapped here for weeks.' Jerry then produced from his pocket the coup de grace. 'And I found this just inside the back door to the Wilson lodge!'

Held in a handkerchief was the stub of a cigar, and on it, plain to see, were spatters of blood.

Tom stood gaping at it, and the others gaped at him.

'Here's what happened. You went to smoke your cigar, and at the same time couldn't keep your mind off the affair going on behind your back. You see Davina leaving the lodge, so you decide to confront Adeyo. But it doesn't go so well. You fight, and in the fight, the stub of your cigar that you had put out and saved in your pocket falls to the floor. Enraged by what this man and your wife were up to, you find something that can hurt him – and whack! You stab him right through his chest! Knowing you don't have long; you leave by the back door. You know you're not meant to be close when Davina screams, so you hide in the shadows while the rest of us come to the lodge. Just as you start to make your way back, you realise you've dropped your cigar butt... that's why you took so long! You suspected that it had fallen somewhere, and you spent all of that time looking for it – but knew you had to get back to Maggie before too long.'

Tom flew from his seat. 'Lies! All lies! I didn't even know they were having an affair!'

'A likely story. Everyone knew about it; this is

a fucking tiny island.'

Tom sprung at Jerry, murder in his eyes. It took all three men again to wrestle him to the floor.

'Lock him up in one of the empty storage rooms until the police get here,' Jerry said as the others dragged the still protesting Tom away.

Jerry went to the drinks cabinet and poured himself a whiskey while the women huddled together and talked the events through. He smiled out of the window – the storm was clearly on the horizon.

While everyone stayed behind, shell shocked at the revelations, Jerry made his way out into the thickening air. He walked to his lodge, the only singleton on the island. So much for a holiday, he thought to himself, his brain already churning away what he'd have to write on the police statements. Getting the blood spatter on the cigar to look just right was the hardest part, but he had to remember that finding it had been a stroke of luck in the first place.

Jerry entered his lodge and couldn't resist taking a peek under the bed. He smiled as he saw all that lovely toilet paper, just for him. So, a man had to die for him to get it, but Adeyo shouldn't have hoarded it in the first place.

Ravenshire

***

Renee Schnebelin

Mrs. Halliday

Sheriff Joseph Henry knew something wasn't quite right when Mrs. Halliday strode into his office this morning smoking a fag. Her lips were pursed tightly around the Virginia Slim as she strode in with a look of worry in her eyes.

"What's the matter, Mrs. Halliday? You've been wandering into my station too much this week. Please don't tell me you lost someone again." The sheriff was trying to be funny, but he knew Mrs. Halliday didn't have anything good to tell him.

Mrs. Halliday owned a small bed and breakfast down on Stone Hollow, The Halliday Inn B&B, and she had been reporting missing guests all week.

Mrs. Halliday took the fag out of her mouth and set it in the ashtray on the Sheriff's desk, "Oh, Sheriff. This time it was just one of them. Room 13 had newlyweds on their honeymoon, just married on the bay last week. The wife walked down this morning in tears saying that her husband just disappeared in the night. They went to bed at the same time – she said her husband kissed her goodnight – and when she woke up this morning, he was gone."

"Maybe he ran off." The sheriff knew better

but had to say it anyway.

"Nah, she said that all of his belongings were still there, keys, wallet, shoes. She said he might have gone out for a soda in the middle of the night, but she just knows he didn't go anywhere. The Mazda is still in the drive and all." Mrs. Halliday put the smoking Virginia Slim back between her lips and took a puff before putting it out.

"Sounds like I should take a drive out and talk to Mrs. I will get a report from her and then we will set up a group to see if we find her husband."

"Thank you, Sheriff. I will meet you at the B & B."

"Just doing my job. Now don't go losing anyone else before I get there," the sheriff laughed as Mrs. Halliday headed out of the station.

The sheriff stood up, put his hat onto his head, and walked over to Corporal Shirley's desk. "Take messages for me until I return. Heading out to the Halliday Inn."

"Another one gone missing?" Shirley asked.

"Another one. I have just got to get to the bottom of this. Do you think old man Kraster might have anything to do with this?" The sheriff previously had run-ins with the Kraster family before and it wouldn't surprise him if they were involved.

"It's worth the drive. You want me to grab Hadley and take a drive out to the Kraster property while you speak with the Mrs.?" Shirley asked.

"Good idea. Two birds, one stone. We need to solve this mystery swiftly before the townsfolk start talking again and stir up some cockamamie story that draws attention to news outlets. Last thing we need is reporters nosing around. I am going to head out. You two be mindful when approaching the Kraster's."

"I'll grab Hadley and we'll do the same. I promise that we'll try to not stir up any trouble. Meet here later or at the B&B?" Shirley asked.

"Here at the station. See you then." The sheriff grabbed his holster on the way out.

The Krasters were one of the original families that had moved to Ravenshire many years ago. They had owned and operated the Kraster Family Farm for generations growing poppy flowers and a bean field. They were also troublemakers who had been part of a few murder investigations. They were not ones to mess with, but if they were involved, the sheriff would be in the middle of a shitstorm: the biggest one Ravenshire had ever seen and it may be the last one at that.

Halliday Inn

Sheriff Joe pulled into the Halliday Inn parking lot to find Mrs. Halliday standing at the top of the steps, smoking another fag.

"You know them ain't any good for you," the sheriff said as he strode towards the foot of the steps.

"Ha ha, Sheriff. Now is not a great time to quit," Mrs. Halliday responded. "Mia is sitting inside; her husband's name is Bradley."

***

The sheriff stepped inside to the bed and breakfast. The bauble wasn't any different than last week. The same weird pink elephant statue stood in the lobby next to the vending refrigerators. He wasn't sure why Mrs. Halliday had put that there, but he would never question her taste. The sheriff also noted that the elephant statue seemed slightly skewed.

"Mrs. Halliday, have you looked at that statue in the last few days?" the sheriff asked.

Mrs. Halliday looked at the statue with a puzzled look on her face. "Huh? It's been moved."

"That is what I thought. Why don't you talk to Mia? Take a statement while I examine the statue." The sheriff had an idea and wanted Mrs. Halliday to keep Mia busy.

"Will do, Sheriff," Mrs. Halliday said as she disappeared around the corner to talk with Mia.

The Tunnel

The Sheriff began to examine the elephant statue and immediately saw that it had been moved. Pushing and pulling on it seemed to do nothing. The sheriff finally realized that pressing the orange soda button on the refrigerator was the key.

The pink elephant moved to the side, revealing a tunnel behind it. The sheriff stepped inside and as soon as he started down the steps, the door behind him slid shut, engulfing him into darkness. The sheriff pulled out his flashlight, turned it on and began to follow the beam of light, assuming that the way behind him was firmly shut.

The tunnel weaved on and on for what seemed to be a mile when he finally found some steps that led to a trap door. Quietly, he walked up the steps and pushed upon the door, which slowly opened into a field. The sheriff peered out and knew that he was looking upon the Krasters' bean field. Straight ahead was the Krasters' main home; to the right was a barn; and the left was the driveway where Shirley's SUV was just now pulling up. Sheriff realized he needed to make his way to the barn. He was sure that was where he would find the missing visitors.

The Barn

Sheriff Joseph Henry never believed his day would end by finding a barn with all of the missing tourists from the previous three months.

After emerging from the tunnel, Sheriff Joseph made his way towards the barn. In his peripheral vision, he saw Shirley and Hadley making their way to the front door. He knew that this would buy him some time.

Sheriff made it to the barn door, pulled it open and what he saw on the other side had him immediately drawing his gun and looking behind him to make sure he hadn't been followed.

Inside the barn, the sheriff found people

fettered, with their mouths taped shut. Most were still standing, but some were lying on the ground in their own filth. The sheriff knew he would have to get these people to safety without the Krasters knowing a thing. The last thing the sheriff wanted tonight was a firefight.

Sheriff Joe found the keys to the fetters hanging on the wall and made his way around, freeing all six prisoners. He told them to be quiet as they would be making their way to the tunnel. All were able to walk on their own, minus one woman whom he had to help.

Amazingly, all of them made the walk through the tunnel swift and quiet. After what seemed to be a long time, the sheriff figured out how to get the tunnel to the B & B to open up. The sheriff and the prisoners were greeted by Mrs. Halliday, an upset Mia, and some of the B & B's staff.

It was a bit of a hassle, but after an hour or so, the missing tourists had been sent on their way with some money to keep them quiet; a radio message had been sent to Shirley to let her know that the Sheriff had solved the investigation; and now it was time for the Sheriff and Mrs. Halliday to sit down and have a drink at the end of a long week.

"Let's keep this town quiet for at least a month. What do you say?" The Sheriff looked to Mrs. Halliday as he took a drink of some sweet tea.

"You know I don't have anything to do with the goings on around this town. One week it's the Krasters, the next week it's the Byrds. I just want to run my business and have the tourists stay, be safe and happy," Mrs. Halliday replied as she sipped on her sweet tea. "Speaking of which, I've got dinner on the stove. You should join us for the night. Next week's problems will wait."

"Yes, Ma'am."

But, the Wolf

***

Melissa A. Bartell

They found her, naked, curled into a protective ball – not quite the fetal position – nestled in between the great roots of a giant tree.

"We're so glad we found you," they said. "Here, put this on."

It was her cape, of course, the red one she hadn't worn since childhood. (And she was quite obviously no longer a child.)   She wanted to shred the thing, but conceding to the cold and their false modesty (for they were looking at her nude form, all of them) she wrapped it around her,   at least enough that her soft, pink parts were hidden from the public eye.

"Were you miserable?" they demanded. "Alone with that creature?"

"No," she said. "He was quite lovely, really."

"But he swallowed you. The woodsman saw it."

"No, he saw what he wanted to see. The wolf protected me from Grandmother's dark beliefs and black magic."

"But he had such big teeth, such demonic eyes – surely you were afraid?"

"No," she said. "He made sure I was warm and dry and well fed. He made sure no danger approached me. My sleep was untroubled."

She didn't tell them that his fur was softer than any of the mink coats the old women lusted after, winter after winter, but never dared to make or buy. She didn't tell them that his thick tail would loop around her wrist when she was frightened, or that he would curl himself around her when the nights were freezing, or below.

She certainly didn't tell them that he wasn't really a wolf at all, but a werewolf, in full control of both form and faculties.

And she absolutely didn't tell them that it was possible she was carrying his child. Or children. Or pups. (Would they be pups? Would it matter if they were?)

She wanted to run back to his - well, lair wasn't really the right word. Cave? Home? Den. Yes... den. Den connoted a safe and cozy feeling, and she had been both, and more.

"But the wolf," she asked, her voice trembling because of her worry for him, "is he unharmed?"

"We couldn't find him," one of the hunters said. "It's like he never existed."

They took her to her mother's home, where she found the woman much diminished. Her father had long since disappeared into the forest. Maybe he'd found a she-wolf companion – they said these things ran in families – but more likely, he'd found a bottle, and a river, and a rock, and would never be seen again.

Pity.

She'd have liked to have words with him. About not telling her that his mother was a dark witch who wanted to lock her up until she was thirty. About not telling her that the forest creatures weren't always dangerous. About not telling her to think first and slash out with her knife second.

She'd cut him. Not her father, but the wolf. She'd drawn his blood while he never drew hers. Well, not with a knife. But she'd been a virgin the first time he'd lain with her, and that kind of bloodstain was better earned.

A week passed, then a fortnight, then a month. On the day after the full moon, he came to her door in human form.

"I love your daughter," he told her poor, insane mother. "I wish to marry her. She's carrying my child."

Her mother approved; the date was set. After the old woman was well asleep, he went to her bedroom.

"I love you." He gave her the words he'd shared with her parents. "I've missed you."

"But, the wolf?" she asked, her hand curving protectively around her belly.

His eyes flashed amber for a moment, then soft brown replaced them. "Oh, the wolf... he loves you too."

Silent Serenade, Silent Night

***

Renee Schnebelin

Once upon a night….

Sophie danced on the beach as a mandolin played in the distance. The water lapped over her bare feet as the tide moved in, sucking her into the sand. As the sun set even further below the horizon Sophie knew what she had to do. As heartbreaking as it was, she had to let him go and finish the job.

Sophie walked onto the pier and headed down to the end. She approached the tarp, and made sure the weights were secure before bending down and pushing the lifeless body into the water. Sophie watched as the figure swirled towards the bottom disappearing into the darkness never to be seen again. Sophie stood back up and walked back down the pier, stepping onto the sand, looking left and right to make sure she hadn't been seen. Thankfully, the beach was completely empty. Sophie smiled as she headed towards the sounds of the joyful mandolin to find her next victim.

Part Three: Loves and Losses

Love

你是我最爱的人

и я верю, что ты меня тоже любишь

But sometimes I think we don't understand each other

Så jeg vil prøve å lære språket ditt

- F. Hood

Death and the Miser

***

Anne-Charlotte Gerbaud

On the 1st day, Luke was visiting the National Gallery of Art in Washington DC when he saw a painting. Luke looked at the note and read: "Hieronymus Bosch – Death and the Miser, c. 1485/1490, oil on panel". He raised his eyes. There was something about the painting: he could not stop looking at the ray of light, the crucifix, the angel encouraging the dying man to look at it, Death at the door, and the demons slowly invading the space. There was also the dying man, tempted with a bag of gold, and the man in green, fingering a rosary while putting coins in a jar kept by a rat-faced demon. There were so many details, Luke was hypnotised.

He sat on the bench facing the painting and kept looking at it. He went back the following day, and the day following the following day, and the day following the day following the following day. Staff in the museum were amused by this bald little man who came to see Bosch's painting.

On the 142nd day, Luke brought papers and pens and started to draw. He was frantic. Pens were running over the blank pages. He was so passionate that even the staff did not want to bother him. He was drawing every detail of the painting: on one page, the crucifix; on another, the skull of Death; on another one, the rosary, etc.

On the 181st day, he did not go to the museum. Instead, he left his house to get paint and blank canvases. Back home, he started to paint. He wanted to create a flawless copy of 'Death and the Miser'. He wouldn't stop until he surpassed Hieronymus Bosch.

He painted for hours. He painted for days. He slowly stopped showering, sleeping, and eating. He could not waste his time with such trivial activities. He had so much work to do and felt feverish just at the thought of the task ahead. He was seeing the demons of the painting walking around his studios and snickering, trying to steal his tubes of paint or his brushes.

On the 201st day, he put the last stroke of paint on the canvas. He stepped back to look at his masterpiece. He had done it. 'Death and the Miser' was facing him. His breath became erratic and he started to sob. He put his head in his hands and cried.

"Well done, Luke," a voice behind him said.

Luke quickly turned round. Hieronymus was facing him.

"This is even better than what I've done," Hieronymus said. "You deserve to rest now. Luke walked over to and embraced Hieronymus who transformed into Death.

On the 202nd day, the body of Luke Taylor was found in his studio located at 1418 Hickory Lane, Washington DC. Around him were hundreds of copies of 'Death and the Miser' by Hieronymus Bosch.

The Golden Hours Rest Home

***

Ann Powell Lewis

All I wanted to do was eat my chicken salad in peace and read my Kindle. Undisturbed. I hate being interrupted when I'm eating, and I hate being interrupted when I'm reading. And I really, really hate being interrupted when I'm eating and reading, which is my favorite thing ever. But the Golden Hours Rest Home was short staffed, as usual, and Ginny, the director had asked me to sit in Miss Viola's room during my lunch break, instead of outside on the bench under the tulip magnolia where I usually took my break.

"I'm begging you, Dara—I just don't have the staff to cover breaks today. Keisha's out post-appendectomy for God knows how much longer, not that I can blame her for that, of course, Stanley's on vacation for five more days, and Tamara—well, you know all about that." Ginny was actually wringing her hands as she delivered this speech.

I always thought hand wringing was something metaphorical, but she was literally wringing her large, red, chapped hands in desperation.

I sighed. The book I was reading was fiction, loosely based on the real life of a woman who had been a spy in occupied Paris during WW2. It was riveting and I'd just reached a chapter where she was going to have to 'compromise her morality', as the book phrased it, with a Nazi officer, or else possibly cause the deaths of innocent civilians. I knew of course that she was going to choose 'compromise' as the lesser of the two evils, but I couldn't wait to read about how it actually happened.

"Okay, I guess," I said. "But only if I stay on the clock—if I can't leave the building, then I should get paid for my non-break lunch." There actually wasn't enough money in the world to compensate for giving up my lovely bench and thirty minutes of tranquility, but Ginny was a good boss, and had always treated me fairly, so I didn't really feel right refusing her. I knew she would have to go sit in Miss Viola's room if I said no.

Ginny heaved a sigh of relief. "Thank you, Dara! I can always count on you."

Miss Viola was one of the sweeter residents at Golden Hours. She'd been here for a little less than a year, ever since she'd taken a fall down the steps at her home and broken a hip. I tell you, whenever someone breaks a hip, it's the beginning of the end. I refuse to live in a house with stairs for just that reason, even though I'm only 32 and not exactly at risk for a broken hip, but I'm not taking any chances. I've seen this story too many times. Person living at home, perfectly fine, independent, and then BOOM. They fall, break a hip, and it's a downward spiral to the graveyard from there on out. Nope. No stairs for me. I live in a little one-story bungalow in my town of Asheville, North Carolina. No steps anywhere, except for the three steps from the kitchen into the garden. And I had handrails installed there and I use them every single time.

Although Miss Viola was a sweet natured little old lady, she had begun to lose her sense of reality since being admitted to Golden Hours. It happens a lot and I can understand why. There you are one minute, living your life in the home you've been in for decades, probably where you raised your family, had pets, cooked dinners and sat in your garden with a glass of wine; and then the next minute, you're being bundled off into a strange place where you have people poking and prodding you, no privacy, everything smells of urine and the dingy corridors are full of old people shuffling aimlessly behind walkers or being pushed along in wheelchairs with nurses speaking to them like they're children—I'd want to check out mentally, too. The reality of the situation is unbearable.

So, Miss Viola had become confused and was prone to climbing over her bed rails and trying to escape. She was probably trying to find her way back to her real home, which sadly, her daughter told me, no longer exists as it was bulldozed to make a parking garage. Is that not the most depressing thing ever? So poor Miss Viola cannot be left alone.

Normally we have an unskilled aide to cover breaks for patients like Miss Viola, but like I said, we are totally short staffed due to a perfect shit storm of events which I won't go into, but I will give you the example of Tamara, just so you have some idea of what this place is like. Ginny is great, yes, but she alone cannot fix the myriad problems that exist at Golden Hours.

So, Tamara (pronounced 'Tah-morr-a'— accent on the second syllable) is a nice girl. She really is. Or was. She doesn't work here anymore, as you may have gathered. Tamara was a registered nurse. We have one on duty for every shift— it's mandatory—because licensed practical nurses like me, and of course the aides, are not allowed to administer medications. State law requires that all medications be dispensed by the registered nurse.

And Tamara was having some 'personal difficulties' as they say. They were pretty major difficulties. She was a single mother with an autistic teenager by one absent father, and a hyperactive three-year-old by another, also absent, father. And she'd just found out she was pregnant by her unemployed meth addict boyfriend. Yeah, she made some bad choices, but who knows at the time that you're making bad choices? It could happen to anyone, but people like to shake their heads like they are so much better and smarter, and they would never end up like Tamara. Me, I know it could happen to me. Although, after hearing Tamara's tale of woe I went directly to Planned Parenthood and had a Mirena IUD inserted.

There is no fucking way I am going to find myself saddled with a couple of mental kids and no dad in the picture. Actually, I'm hesitant even to date anymore, and it's been eight months since I've had sex, so the Mirena is probably redundant, but better safe than sorry.

It gets even worse with the Tamara situation. So, her meth-head, live-in boyfriend somehow got access to her bank account —how that happened, I have no idea. I wanted to ask, but poor Tamara had so much crap raining down on her it seemed in poor taste, so I didn't. This boyfriend cleans out her bank account and spends it all on drugs. Tamara found out when her rent check bounced. So, she got kicked out of her apartment, with the two kids, and had to move in with her divorced alcoholic mother who lives in a trailer way out in the boonies of Leicester County. The mother spends her days drinking Jack Daniels and blasting Def Leppard. Can you even imagine? The autistic teenager sits in a corner banging his head against the fake fireplace and the hyperactive three year old is bouncing off the walls; and the whole time Tamara is at work, she's afraid her mom is not watching the three year old and he might be drowning in the creek that runs behind her mother's single wide; and meanwhile, she doesn't know what to do about this pregnancy. She wants to have an abortion but she's also Baptist and she's afraid she's going to burn in hell if she does.

I said to her, "Tamara, hell could not be any worse than your life right now. For God's sake, get an abortion immediately, today if possible, while it's still early." But Tamara can't make up her mind.

Meanwhile, she's super stressed about money and has the worst possible idea ever about how to get some quick cash. Basically, she fakes the documentation on some patient charts and says that she gave them Percocet or Demerol for pain, and she pockets the drugs and sells them through her meth-head ex-boyfriend who for some reason is also still her boyfriend.

(I'll admit, that right there does indicate a certain mental deficiency on the part of Tamara.)

She told me the whole story when we went out after work to Rocky's Hot Chicken Shack for some wings and a couple beers—mainly to give Tamara the strength to deal with her drunk mother and Def Leppard for the rest of the evening. I didn't know what to say. I wished she hadn't told me. I couldn't snitch on her—she was my friend—but I felt weird having this knowledge, because I just knew—I knew—that she was going to get caught. And she did. And she got fired, and I don't even know where she is now, or what she's doing. She hit me up for a couple hundred and I gave it to her—I knew she'd never pay it back, but I couldn't say no. Besides, she needed it more than me.

So, that's just a little back story on this place, Golden Hours. Have you ever noticed how the names of rest homes or nursing homes or whatever you want to call them are so ridiculously inappropriate? I mean they should be called something truthful, like 'Shithole' or 'If You're Lucky You'll Die Before You Get Here', something along those lines. But no, they call them

'Peaceful Acres', or 'Magnolia Plantation' or in this particular case, 'Golden Hours Rest Home'. Ha! Golden, my ass!

I gently crack open the door to Miss Viola's room. She had a Haldol about an hour ago, so I'm hoping she's asleep and I can read in peace. I tiptoe into the room, and gently close the door behind me. I'm in luck. Miss Viola is flat on her back, her papery old face almost as white as her pillowcase, her mouth open. Her chest is barely rising and falling with each shallow breath she takes. She is wearing an old flowered blouse that is not buttoned all the way up. (I need to speak to the aide about that—how hard is it to do up some buttons for Chrissake?) I can see the outline of her ribs. She's so awfully thin because she hardly eats anything. She has a box of Ensure on her bedside table, but I know from experience that she doesn't like Ensure either. Says it tastes like vomit. That's her description, not mine.

I sit down in the vinyl covered guest chair and start reading. I left my chicken salad in the employee refrigerator because I cannot eat in a patient room. They don't smell too great for one thing and for another it just seems unsanitary. Bedpans and adult diapers and whatnot all over the place. No thanks. The heroine of my novel, Elodie, is a young, blonde 23-year-old who drinks red wine and chain smokes and is drop dead gorgeous. She had a boyfriend, but he got shipped off to fight somewhere and she has no idea if he's even still alive. Her father is dead, and her mother is a cripple living in a basement in the 6th arrondissement, and Elodie is the only way her mother has to get food. So, there's a lot of pressure on Elodie even before she gets a job as a translator for the Germans and catches the eye of a high-ranking German officer. I'm just getting into the part where the officer lets Elodie know—in a manner that sounds quite gentlemanly, but you know that underneath that politeness is a threat, and that if she doesn't sleep with him, there will be ugly consequences—I'm just getting into that part, when I hear the bed squeak.

"What are you reading, Dara? That is Dara isn't it? All you young girls look so similar and I don't know where my glasses are."

This is typical for Miss Viola. Some days, she's completely batty, and other days, she is as sharp as you or me. I sigh. At least I'm on the clock, so I guess I shouldn't really feel resentful about being interrupted. "Hi, Miss Viola. Yes, it's me, Dara. How are you?"

"Oh, I guess I'm fine. How are you? Do you know if my daughter is coming today?"

"It's Wednesday today, and your daughter comes on Tuesdays and Thursdays," I say.

"Sometimes on Saturdays with your grandsons."

"It's so hard to keep track of the days, Dara. Do you have trouble too, or is it just me?" Sometimes these old people will break your heart. I try not to let myself get emotionally attached, I keep a distance, maintain a hard shell. Because who

94

needs more sad emotional drama in their life, I ask you? Nobody, that's who.

"Sometimes I have trouble, too, Miss Viola," I say. I actually don't, unless I had too many beers the night before, but I don't need to tell her that.

"What are you reading," she asks again, peering at the Kindle in my lap.

"Oh, it's about this woman who was a spy in Paris, during WW2." I look at the Kindle in my lap. Maybe I could read aloud to Miss Viola? Entertain both of us? Kill two birds with one stone, so to speak?

Miss Viola seems to perk up. She finds the button to raise the head of her bed and her eyes are actually sparkling when she looks at me.

"I was a spy in occupied Paris, did you know that?" She sounds perfectly coherent, but I can only assume the Haldol is kicking in and instead of making her sleepy, it's sending her off into an alternate reality.

"Umm, no, I didn't know that," I say politely. Just for kicks, I do the math. I know how old she is, and if she had been a spy in occupied Paris (ha ha), that would make her——I have to stop and concentrate because math has never been my strong point—it would make her 96, which, I realize is exactly what age her chart says she is. Just a coincidence, though.

"Yes," Miss Viola continues, warming up to her topic. "My name was Violetta then. Violetta Bertrand. After I married Russell—he was an American GI—I changed my name to Viola.

Easier for Americans to say. I became Viola Smith—Mrs. Russell Smith. But inside, I have always thought of myself as Violetta." Miss Viola is fingering the edges of her ratty old quilt, as if it somehow helps her recall her earlier life. I myself am actually wondering now if this could be a true story? How could she suddenly make this up on the spur of the moment? Miss Viola has never been one to make up stories, at least not that I'm aware of.

"We were hiding a Jewish mother and her baby in our apartment," she continues. My parents had hired her to work for them at the cheese shop they owned. I don't know if she was married or, if she was, what had happened to her husband." She stares out the window at the Canada geese who are eating grass and shitting all over the golf course next door. But she doesn't look like she's actually seeing them. "I didn't want to know anything about her. I was glad we were helping her, on the one hand, because she surely would have been sent to one of those camps and died. Both she and her baby. But on the other hand—I was afraid my family was going to be killed if anyone found out about her."

"Did anyone find out?" I guess that nobody did, or Miss Viola wouldn't be here today.

"No, nobody did, thank the Lord." She smiled. "And then I was told I had to work for the Nazis, translating documents. I was fluent in French, German, and English because my mother was raised on the French/German border and was bilingual, so I grew up bilingual, and I studied English in school."

Miss Viola's eyes cloud over. "What day is it today? Isn't my daughter supposed to be here?" She falls back against her pillow. "I'm so tired."

I am dying to hear the rest of the story. I want to know what she did exactly, as a spy, and if she was forced into any romantic encounters with the Nazis. I want to know what happened to the Jewish woman and her baby. I want to know where she met her husband and if she ever returned to Paris or if she planted her roots here in America and never looked back. But that will have to wait until lunchtime tomorrow because Miss Viola is fast asleep.

Moral support

***

Samia Nicolas

We made it to the audition in good time, I was only there to support my friend Jeremy who, audition after failed audition, had needed a morale boost; so here I was, out of my comfort zone, amongst the luvviest of luvvies I had ever seen and twiddling my thumbs as Jeremy went through his audition piece for the umpteenth time under his breath. I knew it as well as he did now since our shared flat is so small and I was the only one he could ask to practise with; but next thing I knew, he motioned he was heading for the loo and I was there holding his place.

I was minding my own business, peering at the other actors and making swift judgment's about them -   ones I could share with Jeremy in the taxi home to make him feel better -   when a young woman with a name tag that read 'Klerwi' holding a clipboard poked her head through a doorway and called Jeremy's name. I looked towards the toilet but there was no sign of him.   I could see Klerwi moving on to the next name, so (and I don't know why, unless I thought it would waste time until he was back, perhaps) I sprang up from my chair and said that I was Jeremy.

There were three very serious looking people in the room and they didn't say a thing, just looked at me over the tops of their noses, probably wondering why I was flapping around the room like a penguin on speed and not starting the audition piece. I think I commented on the lighting rig and the fact there was a camera and a microphone, and they started to look impatient, so what else could I do but start the speech? I knew it off by heart and Jeremy hadn't shown, and I realised I was the best chance he had.

I felt that confidence you feel when you know a speech off by heart: the words rolling off my tongue like a waterfall; when all of a sudden, my mind went blank. Sunlight had reflected off something and caught my eye, and I froze – the elated feeling I had was transmogrified to lead – all I could think about was that I had screwed up Jeremy's audition big time. Somehow I blurted out the end of the speech, completely made up, words flying out of nowhere -   I think I mentioned a stuffed dog on wheels at some point or other – and I couldn't read the expressions on the people's faces.

I left the room with sagging shoulders, experiencing a snippet of Jeremy's past failures even though this wasn't even my thing. They had said they'd let me know and I was wondering why they hadn't just said no straight away; but, stranger than that, Jeremy still wasn't in sight, so I left the building only to find him standing on the street in tears and blubbering about how he had chickened out.   I never told him what happened, but I guess I'm going to have to soon: my acting debut is next week and I need him to help me learn my lines!

When the Paint Hits the Canvas

***

Thomas Govaers

For Jenny

When the paint hits the canvas, it spreads out easily. She smiles as she sees the canvas take colour. A brush here, a brush there, she's done it a hundred times and it's always so easy to start something new, something fresh. Now it's nothing yet, but she's sure to see a realistic and emotional human face within the hour. She blends as she intends and sends it on its way to give life to this creation. Slowly, the face takes shape: the features start to take form: ears to hear, lips to kiss, eyes to see. It's looking back at her now, lovingly; though the more she works on it, the more it seems to be judging her.

"Why did you paint me like this?" The face intimidates her. "Can't you change my nose? I feel ugly."

"Sure," the painter answers, even though she didn't think it was ugly when she gave the face this nose. "Are you sure you're not happy with your nose?"

"Well," the painting says, "maybe it's my eyes that are misshapen."

"Don't be so cruel on yourself! Would you be happy if I just put a little bit of light in your eyes?"

"Only if it would bring me more to life."

"I think talking is a pretty steady way of knowing you're alive."

"Lots of people that talk seem not really alive."

"You sound older than you are."

"Well, you've created me like this."

"I did, but I didn't really think about what you wanted to be. I mean, you sound like you want to be happy, and I respect that."

"So, what are you waiting for?"

"I thought I could tell you what purpose I had in mind for you, but the choice will be yours."

"Go on, tell me my purpose!"

"I didn't say it was your purpose: I said it was the purpose I had in mind for you."

"Yeah, yeah, tell me!"

"Patience, my dear."

"Please?"

"Ok, my purpose for you wouldn't be to be happy, but rather sad and melancholic."

"What's the purpose in that? I'd rather be happy and alive."

"Well, as you said, a lot of people aren't really living, and the last thing they need is some kind of happy saint that shows them how great everything could be but isn't for them."

"But they get to have the option, right?"

"Yes, maybe, eventually."

"And they look at happy people on their phone for whole days."

"Yeah, but does it make them happy?"

"Probably... Not?"

"No, it doesn't, and that's the point I was going to make. I was going to give you sadness, that would lead to understanding."

"So, why?"

"Empathy is something that brings life to people, real understanding. You can't just make empathy up: you need some sadness for yourself if you want to understand others. I do believe that's what gives life meaning."

"Happiness can give meaning."

"It sure can, but true happiness means you can change something in the world. That creation itself can have a taste of being a creator. That the living being itself can give life to others. If we give it away, it will grow exponentially. That was the purpose I had in mind for you, but the choice is yours."

Roots

***

Maria Claudia Bada

'I am not going, Nan!'.

This time Silvia stated her decision loudly and clearly.

'Eh, our Princess and the Pea! Your cousins from Milan and Rome are all coming with me and your aunties'.

And, as any other time, Nonna Lucietta couldn't really give a damn about her needs.

'Come on, Silvietta, no further discussion with Granny - and we all go this afternoon at the old *casello*.'

'This is our oldest family tradition - and you can't leave Fossacesia without your liquorice roots!'

'But Nan, I have to prepare for my exams…'. Could the call of duty save her a long walk to the riverbanks, in the scorching weather, to end up deeply into mud, smelling of dead jellyfish and cuttlefish bones?

'It's nobody's fault you were so lazy during this summer. And you will not disappoint your granny and aunties! '

Mom smashed an ace. Family duties are the most incontrovertible, especially in the South of Italy.

In this way, Silvia couldn't even say a proper goodbye to her summer boyfriend. Stupid roots!

'*Creatura*, but why are you getting so stubborn?' asked Nonna Lucietta.

'I don't like liquorice, Nan!'

'*Madonna benedetta*, when has this happened? What else do I need to endure? Two wars, nieces divorcing, family broken up and now also this!'

'But Silvia, do you know that we can find ivory there?' Cugino Luca, twelve years old. He loved the story of the White Elephants dead down the river.

'I know, Luca, I can read the Cultural Heritage signs, too'.

So, the story goes that Hannibal, the African king of Carthage, came over to kick the Roman imperial butt, taking thirty-seven white elephants with him from his headquarters in Spain. The African army passed the Alps. In the following fifteen years, they went shitting and resting everywhere, reaching also the riverbanks of Fossacesia - 'where the river marries the sea' as the Tourist Office brags.

'Silvie, did you forget that the roots are magical?' Nonna Lucietta had a past as a midwife without the need of a proper education to qualify for it. She knew everything about herbs and roots, thanks to her own nan, and her great-great-grandmother.

A dynasty of female matriarchal knowledge destined to be forgotten? But not today, not until Granny got her last breath into her lungs.

'We were part of the *concio*, Silvietta. The monks came all the way from Atri, from the mountains down to the coast, to pick up these precious roots and extract the juice'.

Za Celestina had been looking at Silvia in scorn since they started to walk. The old auntie was famed for her ability in crafting from the bark a mind-numbing liquor, universally known as *l'ammazzapreti*.

'You know very well we need to go there before the last tourists' wave,' said Celestina, admonishing the rebel niece with a raised eyebrow.

Bloody tourists!

After the news around the ivory found close to the riverbanks, they came like locusts, destroying the roots.

The heat was implacable. They had been marching for hours in groups of three and four. Finally, they got along a wall of blackberry bushes and ivy.

They needed to stop to pick them up, too, and make a juice to add to the water.

Each year Za Giuli' used the break to gather the youngest around and start his own history lesson.

Silvia overheard his baritone voice from behind the bushes.

'The Babylonians used the liquorice root as a medicine. Alexander the Great brought it here. And during the Middle Ages, the monks made an elixir out of it. And Za Celestina instead makes a killer spirit'. The kids always giggled at this explanation involving their big auntie.

She smiled. Za Giuli' should have pursued a career as an actor, instead of driving trains.

Time to go.

The barky treasure would have been picked, peeled, and sucked to get them all the necessary strength to go back home with bags and bags of it.

The harvest was about to start.

'Look, Granny! The elephant'!

Luca was running back. He always rushed ahead to be the first reaching the banks.

'I saw it, I saw it!'

Silvia couldn't believe her own eyes.

A white, placid Dumbo was approaching their way slowly. What's next? Hannibal's ghost?

Behind, in the glare of the asphalt, glistening muscles were trying to get a van out of the mud 'Circo Ballilla,' shouted Luca, collecting info from a poster hanging on the van's side.

Nonno Mario and all the eldest cousins went to give a hand to the circus people.

The family ended up with free tickets. Silvia smiled again, avidly sucking her deserved root on the way back home.

Part Four: Fantasies and Majicks

Spellbound

In days of old when knights were bold
And kings ruled undefeated,
Then women wise took witches' guise
And healing charms completed.
And majick weaves its wondrous spell
Through history's many pages
As werewolves howl and demons' foul
Escape their silver cages.
Hobgoblins wild and elves and trolls
Cause mischief in our present —
Yet we are blind to faerie-kind
And find such tales unpleasant.
We need to see through children's eyes
Before the majick truly dies.

- J. Andrews

The Witch and the King

***

Anne-Charlotte Gerbaud

Once upon a time, in a land far, far away, lived a woman. She was living alone in the middle of a forest with two cats, Dawn and Dusk. Her house was quite small, with a large room, a bedroom, and a bathroom. The main room was a mess: the shelves were not big enough to contain all the books she had, pots and pans were on the table, and plants were everywhere. She didn't really care about the mess. She actually really liked it.

That woman was a witch. With her books and her plants, she helped the villagers nearby and cured colds, warts, sprained ankles... everything, including broken hearts. She also helped pregnant women to deliver their babies or farmers to grow crops.

People in the village respected her and liked her. They made sure she was safe and gave her food when one of their family members was healed.

Everything was well, until the day the King visited the place and decided he wanted to build a hunting lodge in the forest. On that peculiar day, the King realised that he had to get rid of the witch.

He talked with his private council who told him that it was very inappropriate for a woman to

109

be single, to live alone, and to do the work of estimated doctors without having studied in prestigious universities where women were not allowed. They decided that she was a terrible example for other women, that she was dangerous, and that she had to be stopped.

The witch didn't try to escape. She was brave and was not scared of a bunch of ignorant men. She asked the villagers to take care of her cats, to keep some of her most precious books, and waited for the soldiers to arrive. Villagers tried to oppose the soldiers, but they couldn't do anything. The witch was arrested, and her house was burnt. Seeing the flames devouring her plants broke her heart and she cried silently until they reached the castle.

She was thrown in a tiny cell, deep inside the dungeon.

The King forgot about her and built his hunting lodge. He was delighted but the villagers were not. Without the help of the witch, they got sick and malnourished. Women died in childbirth. Children died of the flu. But the King did not care; he had all he wanted.

In her cell, the witch helped the gaoler to take care of his family and the other prisoners. People came to her, and she would give them a list of plants and instructions so they could make their own medicines at home. She realised that teaching was powerful and that nothing could prevent the spread of knowledge, even bars of a cell.

On a cold autumn day, the single child of the

King got sick. Doctors did not know what to do, and the King was desperate: his son, the heir to the throne, should not die.

The witch heard about the King's son. She asked the gaoler to precisely describe his symptoms. The poor gaoler didn't know and had to ask the hostler, who asked the cook, who asked the maid, who finally asked the nurse who was taking care of the prince. When the gaoler spoke to the witch again, she gave him a recipe that got to the nurse's ears. She was so desperate to look after the dying prince that she tried the witch's remedy.

And it worked. The fever was brought down, and the little prince stood up. Everyone in the court was amazed. The King came to thank the nurse, but she told him that she got the remedy from the maid. The maid told the King that the cook helped her. The cook praised the hostler, and the hostler told the king that the prince would have died without the help of the gaoler.

The King went deep inside the dungeon to find the gaoler and a strange woman who he may have met before but couldn't remember her, so he asked the gaoler who she was. The gaoler introduced the witch to him, and the King was full of remorse. He asked the witch what he could do to repay her, and she asked him to build a school where people would learn about plants and how to use them to heal others.

The King agreed. When the school opened, people came from all over the world to learn from the witch. The villagers helped her rebuild her house, and she lived happily, with her cats, her books, and her plants, for ever after.

What Makes Us Human

***

Jane Andrews

"So, Laura – are *you* going to be able to tell whether you're dating a human or an android?"

The TV presenters' teeth are unnaturally perfect as he smilingly asks the question. He sits opposite Laura, the backdrop behind them both proclaiming, 'The Perfect Partner?' in massive letters. A banner travels across the screen: 'Sponsored by AI Unlimited' The audience waits expectantly.

Laura twiddles a brunette ringlet in her fingers, obviously trying to give the impression of thinking hard – although the whole audience knows this 'reality show' is scripted. "I guess so," she says at last. Turning to face the camera, she laughs. "I mean, how hard can it be, right?"

Larry Loveheart – it's his real name; he changed it by deed poll – winks at the audience. "Well, if AI Unlimited have done their job properly, then you should have your work cut out deciding which of the guys you're going to meet in a few minutes is actually real!" The crowd applauds. "But first, let's remind our audience what you're looking for in the perfect boyfriend..."

He takes a sip of the clear liquid in the glass in front of him as the camera cuts to a pre-recorded segment: Laura is in her bedroom, opening her heart to the millions of viewers she hopes are watching her.

"I want a man who's good-looking, and tall."

"How tall are you?" a voice interrupts.

"Uh, five eight, I think. And he should be intelligent – you know, with a college degree – and be kind to animals and be respectful."

"What do you mean by 'respectful'?"

Laura appears to be thinking. "He should be honest," she declares at last. "I don't want a cheater. And he should treat me like a lady. I'm all for feminism, you know, but I still like it when a man buys me flowers or opens a door for me."

There is some jeering from the audience at this last sentence. Larry Loveheart ignores it, turning to face the camera once more.

"Well, let's see if either of the guys we've brought here tonight are going to live up to your expectations. Let's meet Date Number 1!"

There is more applause as the back-screen splits in half to reveal an aesthetically perfect young man in his twenties. Classically handsome in a blond, Scandinavian type of way, he has several members of the audience literally on the edge of their seats with excitement. As the crowd cheers, he makes his way down the steps towards Laura and then kisses her on the cheek.

"Laura," Larry Loveheart can tell that she likes this one, "Sven is twenty-six, he's a marine biologist and you'll be happy to know he's six feet tall!"

"Can't I just make my choice now?" Laura asks impishly, reading off the autocue.

The audience laughs, but Larry shakes his head.

"No, we're going to let you meet Date Number 2, and that's Marco from Italy!"

Once more, the back-screen splits open and the audience erupts again as a second man descends in Laura's direction. Marco is equally tall and handsome, although this time in an olive-skinned, dark-haired-with-come-to-bed-eyes kind of way.

"Marco is twenty-seven," proclaims Larry. "He's also a male model –" (cue wolf whistles) "with a degree in literature and he owns an Irish wolfhound named Mitzi!"

Laura looks from one man to the other, obviously confused.

"So," Larry remarks chattily, "any ideas at the moment which one of these guys is the real deal, Laura?" Without waiting for a response, he appeals to the audience. "What about all of you? Which one would *you* choose?"

He holds the pause just a fraction longer until the fade to commercial.

*

Audience figures for the pilot episode are phenomenal. Social media is flooded that week with people speculating about which of Laura's dates is really human and which the AI imposter. There's also a lot of interest in just how realistic the android might be. 'Do you think,' tweets one curious fan, 'that their date's over at the end of the evening – or does it go further than that?' The press is equally prurient, hanging outside Laura's flat to see if she's on her own when she leaves for work the following morning and printing obviously posed photos of the nights out. She is snapped with Sven at the cinema and with Marco at a nightclub, and there are pictures of her with both men (although not at the same time, obviously) in some of the most exclusive restaurants, causing bookings to skyrocket.

Laura, meanwhile, feels increasingly more confused. When she is with Sven, she loves the way he listens intently to everything she says, leaning in close, fixing her with those hypnotic blue eyes. His lips when he kisses her are so soft and real that she thinks he must be human; but Marco's lips are just as seductive and his attention equally flattering. One of them has to be a robot – but what if the TV company's just messing with her head and they're both of them real men after all?

*

The second episode sees her back in the studio, flanked on either side by her two dates. She has six weeks to make up her mind, but how can she bear to part with either of them? The audience is also indecisive with half of them rooting for Marco and half for Sven; while the general public has been voting with its wallet, placing staggering bets on one or the other until the bookies stop

116

taking any more wagers.

"So," Larry asks Laura as the camera pans from her to Sven to Marco and then back to her again, "have you decided yet?"

The autocue flashes her prompt. "Do you mean have I decided which guy I want to keep on dating, or which guy's the robot?" she asks playfully.

The audience applauds and there are yells of "Sven!" and "Marco!" in equal number.

Larry settles comfortably into his chair. "Well, let's look at some of your highlights so far..."

A montage of dates flashes across the screen. Laura and Marco walk hand in hand through a park, stopping to gaze at squirrels and delighting over one who boldly approaches them, sniffing at Marco's shoes. They feed ducks; they buy ice cream. The camera pauses as Marco notices a blob of ice cream on Laura's nose and gently kisses it away. The audience sighs, high on romance.

We then see footage of Sven taking Laura to the aquarium, wearing his marine biologist hat as he explains the different species of fish. The audience fidgets slightly, wanting something a little more physical. They enter a room with an enclosure full of rays and Sven shows her how to stroke the delicate, pancake-like creatures. His arm steals round her waist as she does so and the audience sighs once more as he hugs her to him before leaning over and kissing her on the lips.

Episode Three offers more of the same. The audience is becoming ridiculously invested in these characters to the extent that every newspaper every day carries photos and articles about the nation's three favourite people. Meanwhile, someone puts forward the theory that perhaps Laura is the android; and the rumour is fueled even further when the television company declines to comment.

In all this, Laura finds herself fluctuating on a daily basis. When she is with Sven, she thinks he's The One: the perfect boyfriend she's always dreamed of; but the following day, when she sees Marco, she finds herself preferring him. Her emotions are a ping pong ball, ricocheting around in an endless volley for the audience's amusement.

*

By Episode Seven – the final one in the series – she's spent six weeks with Sven and Marco and pre-orders for AI Unlimited's 'Perfect Partner' droid have gone through the roof. She's still no closer to making a decision: she likes both of them, even – dare we use the word? – thinks she may be in love. But tonight, she will have to decide and tell the world not only which man she thinks is a robot but which one she wants to pursue a relationship with.

The opening credits roll across the screen as the camera pans across the studio audience, some waving banners with 'Select Sven!' and others proclaiming, 'Marry Marco!' in large colourful lettering. When it finally rests on Larry Loveheart, everyone leans forward expectantly. The network's promised a big surprise for tonight's finale and they can't wait to find out what it is.

Ever the consummate professional, Larry rattles through his greeting with ease before turning to Laura and giving her an encouraging smile. "So," he says, "it's been six weeks since your adventure started and tonight you're going to tell us which one of these wonderful men is a robot — if you guess right, you win a substantial cash prize and, more importantly, the opportunity to keep the Perfect Partner droid." The audience claps and whistles. "As we all know, the Perfect Partner is the latest in a series of ultra-realistic androids from AI Unlimited, our sponsors for this show. Let's just listen to what their CEO, Martin Jackson, has to say about this product."

In the segment that follows, Jackson explains the rationale behind his company's decision to 'construct bespoke significant others'. "It's all very simple," he says, making direct eye contact with the camera. "You choose your specification and we programme the droid to act in accordance with everything you've asked for. We can include an anti-nagging function, for example, or a romance chip..." (Cue studio laughter.) "...for all those women who're fed up with never receiving cards or flowers on anniversaries or birthdays. Basically, we're giving you all the best bits of someone's personality with none of the flaws. And we're just as careful with the outer packaging too: thanks to a recent technological breakthrough, every droid we make has synthetic skin and body parts that feel and function just like the real thing. In addition, the lithium battery has been adapted to last for seventy years which should be more time than most people need!"

The camera returns to Larry, flashing his impossibly white teeth in a smile that doesn't quite manage sincerity. "So, there you go: The Perfect Partner is exactly what it promises: someone who lives up to all the expectations you've given the company. Laura, let's just remind ourselves what you said you were looking for."

We're back in Laura's bedroom, watching her once more as she specifies a man who's good-looking, tall, intelligent, and respectful. As she repeats the word 'honest', the video clip freezes and Larry turns to Laura, his expression now almost predatory.

"Honesty's very important to you, isn't it, Laura?"

"Well, yes, but..."

"So how would you feel," Larry continues relentlessly, "if I said that one of your dates may – and I have to emphasise that word *may* – have cheated on you this week?"

The audience gasps. Laura's face turns white.

"You said last week that you found it hard to decide, Laura. Well, you have the opportunity now to ask both your dates a question that might help you make that decision."

Laura turns first to Sven. "Sven, have you

cheated on me?" she asks.

Sven looks hurt by the suggestion. "Sweetheart, why would I do that? You know I love you!"

The audience sighs with relief.

She now addresses Marco. "Marco, I'm going to ask you the same question: have you cheated on me?"

Marco's face crumples as he gives his reply. "I'm sorry, Laura. I love you; I really do, but earlier this week, a girl approached me in a bar – you were seeing Sven that night – and..." His voice breaks. "Well, one thing led to another," he finishes awkwardly. "I'm so sorry, but I can't lie and pretend it never happened."

The hurt in Laura's eyes is unbearable as she hears this confession. Meanwhile, the audience starts to boo Marco.

"So, does that make your decision any easier?" Larry asks. "After all, you did say you wanted a boyfriend who was honest – someone who's 'not a cheater'."

"I..." Laura's floundering, but it seems like the surprise isn't over yet.

"We'll be back after the break," Larry announces jovially, "with yet another twist before Laura chooses her Perfect Partner. Stay tuned!"

As the cameras pull back, Laura tearfully faces Marco. "How could you do this to me? I just don't understand."

*

The audience is buzzing by the time the final

segment starts. But then Larry drops his bombshell.

"Laura, you're understandably upset with Marco, but how would you feel if we told you we made him cheat on you?"

"What?" Laura looks confused.

"In fact, we told both your dates to cheat on you this week – as this footage proves!"

In a daze, Laura watches the film that now plays. Marco is sitting in a bar. A pretty girl approaches him and starts making advances. At first, Marco tries to ignore her, but eventually he allows her to sit down next to him and the two share a bottle of wine as they indulge in conversation. She's obviously doing her best to seduce him, but he remains resolute – until the end of the evening when she gets up to leave, then turns and plants a kiss on his lips. The camera zooms in to Marco's surprised expression, then to their lips approaching again. The second kiss lasts much longer, and the audience is obviously expecting him to follow her outside, but instead, he waves her goodbye and she leaves on her own.

"That's how you cheated on me?" Laura sounds amazed. "You didn't sleep with her: you just kissed her?"

Marco nods, looking ashamed. The audience buzzes.

It's now Sven's turn. He's sitting in the same bar, at the same table, when the same girl approaches. The scene plays out like the one with Marco – except when the girl kisses him at the end,

Sven looks around furtively before following the girl outside. Cameras pick out the two of them climbing into a taxi together and disappearing off into the night.

There is a shocked silence. The audience cannot believe what it's just seen.

Laura looks at Sven. "You lied to me!" she accuses.

He looks embarrassed. "I didn't know they were filming."

"But you lied," she repeats.

"Only because I didn't want to hurt you, Babe."

The audience mutters angrily.

"So, Laura..." Larry takes charge once more. "Which one of your dates is the android?"

"Marco," Laura says without hesitation.

"And you've come to that conclusion because...?"

"He was honest with me," Laura declares. Her eyes glisten with tears. "He didn't try to save himself like Sven did – he told me he'd done something wrong, even though he knew it might stop me choosing him as my boyfriend."

"Well, Laura, you're – absolutely right!"

The crowd goes wild.

"So," Larry continues as the noise dies down, "who are you going to choose as your boyfriend? Will it be perfect Partner Marco who'll never lie to you; or love rat Sven who cares more about himself than you?"

The crowd's keyed up for her to say Marco's

name, but when she utters "Sven" there is a chorus of disbelief. Even Larry looks surprised.

"Do you mind telling us why Sven and not Marco?" he asks politely.

Laura sighs. "I think, maybe, I didn't know what I wanted. I thought total honesty was important, but when it comes down to it, I was happier not knowing I'd been cheated on. You see, Sven's lies didn't just protect him: they protected me as well." The audience's outrage rumbles. "AI Unlimited gave me what I thought I wanted," she continues, "but they've given me something I know I can't live up to myself. That's why I'm picking Sven, with his human flaws – I guess I'm just not perfect enough for a Perfect Partner."

Heroism Doesn't Pay

***

Thomas Govaers

Metropolis, a city split between good and evil. Our protagonist today is a superhero and we won't call him by name because he is really modest at those kinds of things. His nemesis goes by the name of Malchus Morte, a highly educated evil villain that is really not particularly creative, but had managed to do his part as antagonist well, until that time.

This particular story starts as a regular day in Metropolis. Malchus Morte had hijacked a civilian aeroplane, full of, you guessed it, civilians. He didn't have a particular purpose with this, except for just being evil. An aeroplane is no match for our superhero though as he cut to the chase. With ease our superhero plucked the machine from the sky, breaking off the wings. The passengers scream in fear, but they sighed of relief when he safely got the tube that was left to the ground. No collateral damage that day because our superhero had always been more professional than other superheroes. With the passengers safe, there was one thing to take care of: Malchus Morte. Call it coincidence: he just climbed on top of the wreckage with a giant plasma gun. That's still no match for our superhero. As soon as Malchus Morte fired his first shot, he got flanked, tackled and disarmed. With that our superhero had sent Malchus Morte into early retirement. The people cheered, the day was saved. Our superhero showed off by flying a couple of runs just above the crowd and they loved it. They cheered and cheered crying tears of joy as if this wasn't an everyday occurrence in Metropolis.

The rest of the day passed without incident and our superhero went to bed early. The next day he was eager to save the city and flew around in the morning to find out what the next evil scheme would be. Nothing happened though. Our superhero, reviewing the events of the day before, thought to himself: "Have I literally send Malchus Morte into early retirement? And I mean literally." You see, Malchus Morte, evil as he was, used an intellectual trick to save up lots of money to be able to have a passive income. They say: 'crime doesn't pay' and they're most definitely talking more about petty thieves because Malchus Morte was a rich son of a bitch. Literally. You don't want to meet his mother.

With Malchus Morte out of business, our superhero was free to do whatever he wanted, well, within the moral bounds of a superhero. The first few weeks were amazing, just hanging out on the beach, destressing with a cocktail in a hammock. But then he started noticing this empty feeling. He needed to save the city! But from what? Crime rates were at an all-time low, because of the monopoly Malchus Morte had created nobody had even thought about pursuing crime. Our superhero even tried to help an old lady cross the street, but was soon chased away by a mob of young boys because they found it their job to help old ladies and saw him as a threat to their job security. They were right, he thought while dropping on a park bench, feeling there is no purpose left for him.

So, what could we learn from this tragic story? Calling someone a hero is used as a substitute for not paying them well. Our superhero didn't have enough savings to go into early retirement himself. But his resumé is only fit for defeating evil villains and without a nemesis, he doesn't have any means to get to work. He doesn't have any other job experiences or degrees. He's heard about his colleagues in other universes and dimensions, that have to take on a civilian job, in let's say journalism or science, just to make ends meet. I don't want to get into politics too much, but we have to admit that this is a huge elephant in the room. Superheroes are a minority movement that protects us against all kinds of evil, but who's protecting the superheroes? Without purpose in life, our hero spiraled into depression and mental illness. Eyewitness accounts say he resides with the seagulls these days, but who knows? Maybe he will return when the city needs him again. Until then, this is where our story ...ends.

Night Vision

***

Jane Andrews

Sasha stared at the email in front of her: "Your training will be complete," it read, "once you have successfully carried out the night duty assigned to you by your commanding officer."

She sighed as she read the words. It seemed that policing was less about using her considerable intelligence to solve crimes and more about pounding the streets, keeping an eye open for any would-be hooligans. Still, if it was a requirement...

"What you got planned for tonight?" Dev's voice intruded on her thoughts. "Only, I was thinking of popping by 'The Stag' later, if you're interested?"

She *was* interested: Dev was probably one of the best-looking guys she knew and he actually had a sense of humour – something that was in short supply at her local police station. Tonight was not the night for such an assignation, though. "Sorry." She tried to put as much regret as she could into her voice. "I'd like to, but I already have plans."

Immediately the words left her mouth, she could have kicked herself. Why hadn't she said she had police work to do? Now Dev would think she had a date with someone else. Okay, so the email had been marked 'Highly Confidential' and it had stated, most explicitly, that she was to **tell no one** (bold font, heavily underlined) where she was going or what she was doing, but surely that didn't include Dev? He might be a slightly newer recruit than she was, but he'd already impressed half her work buddies with his ability to remain calm in a crisis and his uncanny knack of rooting out bad guys, almost as if he could smell the guilt dripping off them.

"Some other time, then." Dev flashed her a brilliant smile that showcased his gleaming white teeth perfectly.

"Yeh," she replied automatically, her mind already moving on to wondering who would walk the dog if she was stuck here all night on secret police business. (If only she'd known beforehand, she could have brought Benji to work with her and walked him as she patrolled.) "Let's definitely do it some other time."

*

"Okay." Julie led Sasha through a door marked 'No Entry' and into a room she'd never visited before. "This is where we kit you out. You'll need a pair of these."

"Night vision goggles?" said Sasha with surprise. "Why on earth would I want those?"

Julie lowered her voice. "What you're about to embark on is Special Ops patrol. You've read Harry Potter, haven't you?"

"Well, yes," admitted Sasha, "but..."

"And you know that there's a hidden

wizarding world that Muggles can't see?"

"Yes, but..."

"Well, J K Rowling didn't make any of that up!" hissed Julie. "At least, she did – but she got the idea from the Undercover Crime Department. When we patrol at night, we're keeping an eye on the hidden world of magic – the one most people think doesn't really exist."

"But it doesn't exist!" Sasha wanted to say. She was beginning to wonder whether Julie was fit to hold such a superior position within the station. Perhaps she should request a psychiatric evaluation?

But there was no time to worry about any of this now. Julie was pushing her towards a gigantic guy in uniform who wouldn't have looked out of place at a Giants' Convention – if giants existed, of course. "Merv, Sasha's your partner for this evening. It's her first time out, so break her in gently."

"Hi." Sasha held out her hand but Merv ignored it. "So," she continued, beginning to babble nervously, "Merv – is that short for Mervyn, then?"

"Mervatroyd," grunted the Neanderthal.

Was that even a real name? wondered Sasha.

"You're gonna need ter put 'em on," he said next, pointing at the goggles. "Yer won't see nuffin' wivout 'em. All the magic stuff that's hidden, that's why you wear 'em."

"But you're not wearing any!" she pointed out, not unreasonably.

Merv sighed. "Don' need 'em, do I?" He glanced at Julie. "Boss, tell 'er 'ow it works."

"Merv's a half-breed," Julia mouthed at her. "He can see the hidden world because he's part of it himself."

"I don't think we're supposed to say 'half-breed' anymore," Sasha began sanctimoniously. "It's 'persons or entities with some magical ability'."

"So you admit magic exists then?"

Damn! She hadn't thought of that. "What exactly are you then, Merv?" she said at last. "Half-man and half-what?"

"Put the goggles on!" Julie said sharply. "It's a lot easier than explanations."

Sasha pulled the device over her eyes and gasped. In Merv's place stood – or rather lurched – a hulking great beast that was vaguely human in shape but far uglier than anything Sasha had ever seen. Its limbs were like twisted tree trunks and its skin was a horrible greenish grey, offset by a bulbous nose and disconcertingly red eyes.

"What is it?" Sasha gasped in horror.

"*Merv*," Julie emphasised his name, "is part-man, part-Troll – and one of our finest officers. And *you* will be keeping him company this evening."

Sasha thought longingly of 'The Stag' and Dev, then looked at the slime dripping from Merv's nose. "Okay," she said at last, "but I hope you've got a good supply of tissues because I refuse to look at snot when I'm on duty."

*

As they began to walk down the street, Sasha knew she had to ask Merv the question that was burning a hole in her brain.

"Merv," she began hesitantly.

"Yeh? Wha' choo want?"

"Well, Julie said you're half and half..." She paused delicately. "Which of your parents was human?" she said at last.

"That was my dad," Merv said reflectively. "He wasn't much to look at, but 'e 'ad a good 'eart. 'Sno wonder me muvver fell fer 'im, even though she could've 'ad anyone she wanted. Now, she was a real beauty..."

Sasha gave an almost imperceptible snort of disbelief.

"Troll women are known fer their pulchritude," Merv said sternly. "Once me dad saw 'er, there was never anyone else – not as far as 'e was concerned. She always said she was glad I took after 'er and not 'im."

Sasha listened with only half an ear. Her goggles were really most uncomfortable. She took them off, wondering if she could adjust the straps.

She was still fiddling with them when Merv let out a roar. "Clear off, yer dirty creature!"

Looking up, she realised that he was running towards a beautiful unicorn. Its white coat glistened in the moonlight and its golden horn shone. A mini-skirted woman – presumably on her way home from some nightclub – was stroking the

132

creature's nose and babbling something about how she'd always known it was true. It seemed unfair of Merv to chase her away, but Sasha supposed he knew what he was doing.

Or did he? She watched in horror as Merv pulled out a nasty looking knife and plunged it into the unicorn's pure, white throat.

"What are you doing?" she screamed in horror, already mentally filing the report that said the Troll had gone berserk and slaughtered an innocent magical creature before she could stop him.

"Put them goggles back on!" thundered Merv.

Sasha did as she was told and felt her stomach turn over. In place of the unicorn stood a maggot-infested corpse of a horse. Patches of its black hair still clung to its emaciated frame and flaming eyes rolled in their sockets.

"What is it?" she whispered, askance.

"It's a Nightmare, innit?" Merv seemed matter of fact. "Come out to prey on anyone oo's stupid enuff ter fall fer that unicorn malarkey. S'all a glamour, innit? The white coat ... the golden horn ... load of old bol..."

"Yes, yes," Sasha said hastily, "I can see that now. But how did you know it wasn't a real unicorn?"

Merv looked at her pityingly.

"There's no such fing as a 'real unicorn'. 'S all just a disguise that Nightmares wear."

"But there must be!" she said in surprise. "I mean, there are books and paintings and... and some children's parties have unicorn rides..." Her voice tailed off uncertainly.

"Unicorn rides!" Merv echoed bitterly. "They'd be better off letting their kiddies swim in a shark tank!"

"And you're telling me that Nightmares are creatures, not just bad dreams?"

Merv nodded slowly. "Now you're getting' it," he said as if he thought she was very stupid. "Nightmares and Gremlins – they're bad; Pixies are just annoying; and Fairies ..."

"Don't tell me," Sasha interrupted. "Fairies are evil and nothing like the pretty creatures you see in children's storybooks."

"Well," Merv considered, "it depends, don' it? Graffiti Fairies – yer wanna stay clear of them. But Washing Up Fairies – they're a different matter entirely." His voice became wistful. "Everyone would love a Washing Up Fairy, or a Cleaning Sprite – but yer hardly see any of 'em around these days. I blame it all on Brexit."

"Sorry?" What on earth had politics got to do with magical creatures?

"Can't get the visas these days," Merv explained sadly. "They're all French Polish, yer see. An as fer the Gnome Anaesthetists... Well, all them cuts to the National Elf Service were bound to 'ave an effect on the otherworld staff. Is it any wonder the country's in such a state?"

It was just her luck to be lumbered with a woke Troll! Sasha thought. Still, at least he wasn't trying to get rid of her. Keeping her goggles firmly in place, she trotted beside him, eyes constantly roving for Graffiti Fairies or Leprechauns.

"Erm, we arrest Leprechauns, don't we?" she asked, checking for clarification.

"Only when they're drunk and disorderly," Merv told her. "It's Boggarts that are the worst when it comes to closing time – they drink far too much and start rampaging through the streets, knocking everyone's bins over."

*

For the next hour or so, they made a systematic sweep of the surrounding streets, breaking up a fight between a Kobold and a Kelpie, and arresting a dozen singing mice who insisted on disturbing the peace. Sasha found she was getting used to the goggles – in fact, after a while, she almost forgot she was wearing them; and when Merv suggested stopping off for a kebab, her excitement knew no bounds.

Despite the lateness of the hour, there was quite a crowd at the counter. Merv motioned to Sasha. "Why doncha' take a seat? Yer've been on yer feet a while now."

It was not until he said it that she realised how weary she felt. She sank down gratefully onto the red plastic bench. "Garlic mayo and chili sauce on mine," she murmured before leaning back and closing her eyes.

She let the gentle hum of customer conversation drift over her while she thought about the evening. Although she would have enjoyed an evening in Dev's company, with perhaps a glass or three of prosecco to help her unwind, she couldn't pretend she hadn't had fun with Merv, learning about the hidden world she'd never realised existed. She should really have taken off her night vision goggles, but she was so tired, and it seemed like such an effort to remove them...

Suddenly, the room fell quiet. Sasha swiveled in her seat to see what had caused the drop in the noise and felt her heart clench as a huge, ugly looking – thing – almost as large as Merv pushed his way into the kebab shop. By her side, Merv froze with the kebabs still in his hand. "You don't wanna get on the wrong side o' one o' them," he breathed. "It's an 'Obgoblin, that is."

"Can everyone else see him?" Sasha felt puzzled. "Only, I was wondering why they've all gone quiet."

"I 'spect that'll be the gun 'e's wavin' around," Merv said matter of factly. "No one else in 'ere can see what 'e really looks like – to them, 'e's just a guy with a weapon."

"So, are we going to arrest him?"

"I fink that might be a good idea," Merv said gravely. Dropping the kebabs on the table, he whirled round. "P'lice! Put yer 'ands up now!"

The Hobgoblin shot Merv a filthy look and made a run for the door. Without pausing to take off her goggles, Sasha reacted instinctively, extending her arm and tasering the lumbering creature as it moved past her. It sank to the ground instantly and lay there twitching.

As Merv struggled to get a pair of handcuffs around the Hobgoblin's hairy wrists, Sasha became aware of how quickly her heart was beating. Adrenaline coursed through her as she became aware that she had tackled something several times her own size on her own. So this was what policing was all about!

"Yer might wanna take yer goggles off an' see what 'e really looks like," Merv instructed. There was a pause before he added poignantly, "*You* can remove yer filter – *I* can't."

Pulling off the equipment, Sasha found herself staring into handsome features she recognised. Who would have thought that Dev Patak was a Hobgoblin?

"He's one of ours," she said tersely. "One of the police cadets, I mean."

Merv nodded sadly. "Happens every year – there's always one or other 'oo tries ter infiltrate us. 'Ow do yer fink I ended up becomin' a p'lice officer meself? Only, I saw the error of me ways an' decided it was a job worf doin' properly."

Dev was slowly coming to. "Sasha?" he said, a little uncertainly. "What you doing here, Babe?"

Once more, he flashed those brilliant teeth, but this time Sasha wasn't fooled. "I know what you really are," she hissed at him. "And I don't like being lied to."

"Did I ever tell you I wasn't a Hobgoblin?" he asked.

Sasha turned to Merv. "Let's get him back to the station."

There would be other good-looking police officers who invited her out – and in future, she would look at everyone with her night vision goggles before she let her heart get involved.

Polite Conversation

***

Jane Andrews

Sidney was the only one who could see the elephant in the room.

All around him, people sipped wine or nibbled hors d'oeuvres, grateful for their first opportunity to mingle in a social gathering (whilst retaining a 2 metres distance from anyone else of course). Conversation ranged from the usual banalities concerning the weather ("So hot ... Marvellous for the strawberries ... Could do with a bit of rain now, though"), family life ("Of course, the kids are completely feral by now after missing so much school – every day, I feel us getting closer and closer to a 'Lord of the Flies' scenario in which they start hunting me or their mother and then sacrifice us to the God of the PS4") and those snippets of personal information that really shouldn't be shared anywhere ("Took me ages to find my bra this morning – it's the first time I've worn one in months!"). In fact, everything was being discussed apart from the very obvious elephant that was standing by the food table and surreptitiously hoovering up all the crab cakes.

"Have you seen that elephant over there?" he asked a Yummy Mummy who was obviously relishing the opportunity to escape the house now that Portia and Tarquin were back in school.

"Don't be silly," she replied, tossing her head so that her immaculately straightened, highlighted locks bounced engagingly. "What would an elephant be doing at an event like this? It's not the London Zoo!"

For a couple of minutes, Sidney observed the other guests. No one was taking the slightest bit of notice of the apparently uninvited guest. He felt a sudden affinity with the creature: after all, wasn't this how he, Sidney, felt at most of the parties he went to? He seemed to have spent a lifetime of standing on his own in a corner, desperately wishing that someone would talk to him.

"Why is everyone ignoring you?" Sidney asked as he wandered across to the food table to investigate a dip in a suspicious shade of yellow.

The elephant regarded him pityingly.

"I'm not a real elephant, you know," it said gently.

"Oh?" said Sidney.

"For one thing," explained the elephant, "I'm pink; but the real reason is because I'm a metaphor."

"I see," said Sidney – although he didn't. He searched his mind frantically, trying to remember what a metaphor was.

"Although," the elephant sounded thoughtful, "I suppose you could say I'm really more of an idiomatic phrase."

Sidney was none the wiser.

"When people talk about 'the elephant in the

room'," the pachyderm continued, "they normally mean something that's obvious but remains untalked about – usually because social etiquette demands that we don't mention anything embarrassing, controversial, inflammatory or dangerous."

"So what are you a symbol of, then?" Sidney wanted to know.

The elephant lowered his voice confidentially. "Have you noticed," he murmured, "how much wine people are drinking?"

"It's a party," Sidney said, puzzled. "An official End of Lockdown Party, to be precise."

"Yes," agreed the elephant, "but don't you think everyone's knocking back a lot more booze than they used to? Let's face it: pubs and restaurants have been closed for months; people have been confined to barracks, as it were, for just as long; all social activities have had to cease – what else has there been for people to do?"

"Lots of people have taken up new hobbies," Sidney suggested.

The elephant snorted derisively. "For most of them," it said darkly, "that involves studying the effects of alcohol at 9 am."

"I think you're being a bit unfair," Sidney protested.

"Look at it this way," the elephant continued. "If you were stuck at home with your children all day, every day, day in, day out – without being able to take them to Soft Play or let them go paint-balling or go-karting, don't you think *you'd* find yourself reaching for a bottle a lot more frequently — just to take the edge off?"

Sidney had to admit that the elephant was right.

"And that's why I'm here now," the creature said with a sigh. "Every single one of them has probably consumed more alcohol in the past three months than they did in the previous three years — but is anyone going to admit that? Of course not! It's like the way people lie on their CVs and claim to have a First in Classics from Oxford when really all they got was a Third in Parks and Recreation from Huddersfield University. Or the way that parents try to outdo each other when they boast about little Jonquil walking at seven months or painting the Sistine Chapel when she was still in her pram — and then you look at the child when she's in the park one day and realise she's the one eating bogies and running into trees like a complete lunatic."

"Okay," Sidney shrugged, "so we're all a bit economical with the truth from time to time — but I don't see why that should cause an imaginary elephant to appear at a party."

"Haven't you wondered," mused the elephant, "why you can see me but no one else can?"

Sidney took a few minutes to contemplate this question and had to admit he was stumped.

"The answer," said the elephant impressively, "is that you're the only one who's being honest. They could all see me if they wanted to — but then they'd have to admit they're a bunch of shallow dipsomaniacs who have a rather volatile relationship with the truth. You, on the other hand, are just as shallow and just as much of an alcoholic — but at least you're up front about it."

"Thanks," said Sidney, trying to work out whether or not this was a compliment.

"Anyway," the elephant said, demolishing the last of the sausages on sticks and turning its nose up at the coleslaw, "I suppose I'd better go."

And with that, he disappeared in a puff of green smoke.

"Did nobody see that elephant?" Sidney appealed to the room in general. Despite what the creature had told him, he felt sure that there must be another person in the room who would confess to having seen it.

His question was met with averted eyes and silence.

Sidney sighed and helped himself to another glass of wine, wondering if anyone would talk to him at all now he'd said that. He looked at his watch. Perhaps it was time for him to leave too.

"Mad as a box of frogs, that one," he heard someone say as he headed for the door, "-only we don't like to talk about it."

Part Five: Ups and Downs

Letting Go

From birth to death,
From womb to tomb,
We face the fight alone.

From infancy to senility,
From nappies to incontinence pads,
We cry ourselves to sleep.

From conception to cremation,
From first kiss to last breath,
We cling to those who remain.

From mother's milk to intravenous drip,
From first dance to last laugh,
We fight to stay alive.

From ups to downs,
From smiles to frowns,
We tread the boards but once.

- J. Harper

Torn

***

Florence Hood

I own two pairs of pink, satin ballet shoes.

One pair is almost pristine. I only wore them for one exam before I stopped dancing. They still have their ribbons on; I was saving them for the next exam. Normally, we have to buy a new pair for each exam, but these were so close to still being perfect that my teacher thought I could get away with it.

The other pair is almost grey now. There are smudges of black and tears in the pleats below the toes. There's actually quite a large hole in one of them. Their ribbons have been swapped for elastic, and they have been used for countless ballet classes. These are the shoes that make me feel like a dancer. These are the shoes that show how many hours I have worked for a craft.

Most people wear leather shoes to class. They last longer and stay looking neat. Black leotard, white-pink tights, black shoes. All of us identical. But I loved my torn satin shoes. They fit so differently. Wearing them, I felt like the princesses in that fairy tale who escaped every night to dance until their shoes fell apart. I stood up straighter in those shoes. I could kick higher, withstand more pain with an elegant expression on my face. I loved them.

The real effects of an adolescence dedicated to dance aren't as visible as tears in pink satin. My feet crunch and crackle in the morning when I wake up. I have calluses and one of my toes won't straighten anymore and bends at an odd angle. I might have broken it at some point. My toenails no longer grow properly; they have been cracked so many times. My hips hurt. All of my joints suffered from such an intense workload while being severely underweight. There is something wrong with my lower back. Mirrors, especially while naked or in tight clothes, make me nervous. It's the intentional legacy of a ballet teacher who used to make us perform in front of mirrors and make us see our fat shaking. Sometimes I catch myself having a mug of hot water for lunch and pretending it counts as soup.

I am better now. I can touch my toes, sometimes, and I don't always hate my cellulite. I do exercises for the pain, and I eat bread with copious amounts of butter. Those pink satin shoes, torn and discoloured, are the most beautiful things I own.

Bless You

***

Beth Collins

She was sitting at the top of the stairs with her face pressed against the smooth, hard corners of the bannisters. When she went to sleep that night, she would still have the lines, pink and strange, on her cheeks. She was trying to squeeze all her sobbing fury through that gap and down to her mother in the kitchen.

"Muuuuuuummy!" she wailed. "MUMMY" she screamed in her most ear splitting, most shrill squeal.

She was one of three women: one thirty-six, one nine and one four. The smallest, she was making all the noise: the only noise in the house. Everything else was a taut and fragile silence.

"Muu-uu-uuu-mmy!"   she   wailed. "MUMMY!"

She was sitting at the top of the stairs because she was in trouble. Because she deserved it.

The silent house contained few valuables. Nothing much precious or sentimental. Nothing much at all. The three did not plan to stay here long. It was a stop on the "adventure", as Mother had called it. But it was really an escape. It was an escape from silent, creeping evil that had made a permanent mark on one of the three and was reaching to the next at the moment when they had

147

run.

"One bag each," Mother whispered, "and you can choose one thing, a treasure. I'll pack the rest."

The little - screaming - girl could just see it from her seat at the top of the stairs and it made her cry even harder. Her mother's one treasure.

She *should* cry: she was guilty.

It was Mother's mother who had made it, an unknown woman to this little girl. She had sewn it in tiny, girlish, wobbling stitches. The colours had now faded and the cloth become tinged so that the whole thing was mostly beige and brown - or had been.

"Muuuuuuummy!" she wailed, "MU-U-U-UMMY!" she sobbed.

It wasn't very pretty, but Mother had always kept it safe - the last reminder of a happy childhood. A safe and happy time. It had been hidden out of harm's way in the last home; the one they had run from with just three treasures, a little money, and a lot of hope.

It should have stayed hidden away, then she wouldn't have ruined it. But Mother had taken it out to air on the line.

"So, it's fresh and lovely to hang above your bed," Mother had said. "You'd like that, wouldn't you?"

Bless you, baby Jesus
and
Please God, bless this house

148

No-one in the house believed in the words, but the sentiment was comforting, and the love stitched into the plain and delicate fabric meant something powerful to Mother.

"Muuuuuuummy!" she cried, "Mummy - mummy - mummy - mummy..." she begged.

She had never been told off like that before. Mother's face had gone white and purple with shock then rage when she saw the thin and fragile scrap of cloth on the ground. That was bad enough, but the horror - it was almost completely soaked through with the sickly yellow paint. Paint from the tin that was on its side, on its side on the ground. On the ground next to the little easel. The little easel that she was painting on with the yellow paint. The yellow paint they had found in the funny, tiny cupboard under the stairs. The special yellow paint from under the stairs, that the adults had used to paint the bedroom walls. The special paint that was for adults, that she had been allowed to use with her brightly coloured brushes. The special paint for a special girl.

But she wasn't special anymore. She was a naughty, naughty, nasty girl who was careless and shouldn't have treats. She was a careless girl who had tipped over the paint and hadn't picked it up. She hadn't picked it up and she hadn't called Mummy, the naughty, naughty girl.

And so, the wind had stolen the thin, plain, delicate, fragile, beloved scrap of stitching and had landed it in the pool of paint.

And it was ruined.

Mother went on and on with rage and grief. She was so desperate at the loss of the final scraps of her safe and happy childhood. She was so quick and rough with getting her - already crying - smallest girl inside the house and up the stairs where she "would stay until she had learned the lesson!" She was so quick and rough and loud and cross that she did not see her other girl out in the garden.

There was another girl, nine years old, in the corner of the garden. Beside her was a bright red football.

And was that a smear of yellow on the side of that bright red ball?

A sickly smear of sickly yellow. A silent mother and a sobbing child.

Bless you, baby Jesus
and
Please God, bless this house

Never Wade While Wearing Velvet

***

Melissa A. Bartell

She wasn't born in the water, but she feels the ebb and flow of the tides in her veins. She knows the feeling of damp sand under her feet better than she will ever understand the sensation of walking on a sidewalk, wearing shoes.

Shoes seem so wrong.

The beacon from the lighthouse was her night light as a child. Her protector. No monster, no demon, no ghost, could tolerate the periodic brightening of her room. She used to check the shadows to be sure.

The big house on the cliff was a place she used to fantasize about, lying on the sand, the ends of her hair spread out around her, dangerously close to the nibbling waves, feet pointed up the hill, tan, sandy, pink toenails contrasting with the colors of surf and shore.

She never expected she'd marry into the family that owned the place when she was a girl, imagining what went on behind those brightly lit windows.

That shadow crossing the top floor windows must be a ghost... She walks back and forth every night.

I think that's The Boy's room. I saw him on the beach the other day... he and his father were launching their catamaran. I saw the shadows of airplanes hanging from his ceiling. I love that he has planes like I have mermaids.

His mother always looks so formidable, with her perfect hair and perfect sunhat; I bet she even has a perfect rocking chair where she sits in front of a perfect fire.

Life goes on, as it always does, rising and falling like sun and moon, the wind, the ocean waves. She morphs from a child to a girl to a young woman. The Boy from the big house becomes a friend, then a date, then a lover.

He brings a midnight picnic to the hollow behind the sand dunes, where they can see the water but cannot be seen by anyone who might be walking the beach in the moonlight.

The ring he offers is tasteful, delicate.

"It belonged to my grandmother," he tells her. "She died in a fire at the old inn... the one they're razing to build condos... but her fingers had grown too gnarled for the ring. It's not from a corpse – I swear. She'd have liked you."

She smiles and accepts the ring, the proposal, the promised future.

She likes the way his kisses taste like salt-water taffy, and the way he's totally comfortable in rolled-up khakis and a chambray shirt, sitting on the sand near a bonfire, and equally comfortable dressed in a coat and tie and shoes (she still hates shoes, but she wears heels because they're better for dancing) that gleam from shining.

She loves the way his brown eyes hold secrets only for her, and the way he shivers when she teases the nape of his neck with bunny kisses. She loves the way his lean, athletic body (he lettered in crew and baseball) fits with hers.

Their first time was *not* on the beach – beach sex is much less romantic than it sounds; sand gets in all kinds of uncomfortable places – but it was illuminated by the lighthouse's beacon, which visits his bedroom, just as it always visited hers.

At their wedding, she wears a gown of silk velvet, but her hair is down, and instead of a veil she wears a ring of flowers with a few seashells sewn in. She threatened to go barefoot but found pale gold sandals and wore those instead.

He vows to support her art, her music, her writing.

She promises to support his sailing and toy making – the airplanes from his room have become more than a boy with a balsa-wood kit; rather, they are now his livelihood.

They agree that if children come, or if they don't, they'll be equally happy.

As soon as the ceremony is over, she kicks off her sandals. Their first dance is on a wooden floor embedded in the sand, and the crashing waves feel like an integral part of the music.

Champagne goes to her head. She is giddy, joyful, invulnerable. She scampers back and forth at the water's edge, flirting with the foam, letting the cold Atlantic kiss her toes the same way The Boy – now Her Husband – kisses her lips.

When she stumbles, he is there to catch her, bring her away from the surf. "Never," he tells her, "wade while wearing velvet. It soaks up the water, becomes heavier than lead."

She nods blindly. Her head is swimming. Surely, she wasn't in that much danger?

Years fly by. For their thirtieth birthdays, they spend a week in Belize, sailing and snorkeling. For their fifteenth anniversary, they leave their seven-year-old daughter at home and spend a week in the keeper's cottage of a lighthouse in northern California.

When their daughter turns eighteen, they rent a yacht and tour the Caribbean for a month before sending her off to her ivy league university.

But the Caribbean, the Pacific, these waters are not home.

At their daughter's wedding, she again wears velvet, but this time it's not white but the color of coffee and cream.

She still kicks off her shoes as soon as the ceremony is over.

And she still gets too drunk from just a few sips of champagne.

She wasn't born in the water, but the undertow catches her skirts, and she dies there, no longer a young girl with a lifetime of possibility ahead, but still too young for it to be over.

They fill her casket with shells and dried flowers, so the scent of the sea will always be with her. And The Boy – The Man – Her Husband – Her Widower – slips a piece of saltwater taffy between her lips before they close the lid – to remember him.

The beacon from the lighthouse was her night

light as a child. Her protector. No monster, no demon, no ghost, could tolerate the periodic brightening of her room. She used to check the shadows to be sure.

Well... *most* ghosts.

Because now that she's dead, the beacon is her chariot, carrying her into the room that was once hers, and where now a strange child sleeps. She soothes a nightmare away with a cool hand and promises that the light will keep him safe.

She visits the attic workshop where her husband, the toymaker, is creating models of lighthouses that really light up.

She sits on the window seat in the bedroom that used to be his but is now where their granddaughter sleeps when she comes for the summer. All strawberry braids (like hers) and dark eyes (like his), the child loves the sea and makes wishes on the lighthouse beacon.

The strawberry child never knows that her grandmother really *is* there with her in spirit.

But when she meets The Girl from a few houses down the cliff, the one who always smells like ships and tar and adventure, she decides to wear the silk velvet gown that her mother, her grandmother also wore.

And she promises her grandfather, gravely, with dark eyes wide and luminous, that she will never, *ever* wade while wearing velvet.

In Such a Dream

***

Florence Hood

I often think about my children.

I know, I know, it's just the syndrome. But I do. I remember them.

I had a minor head injury, and while I was out cold, I experienced hallucinations. I know this. Logically, I know this. But those hallucinations felt real. Calling them hallucinations feels like lying.

When I came to, in my head, I had lived decades. I was married, I had children – George, my eldest, he and his girlfriend were expecting their first baby – I had a whole life. And then... Back. Back in my twenties, as if none of it had ever happened.

Because it hadn't.

I feel utterly unmoored. The floor dropped out from under me. There is a hole in my chest. When I roll over at night, I reach out to where Beth should be and jerk awake when her side of the bed is empty. My wife doesn't exist, and I grieve for her every day. I get annoyed at my children for not calling to tell me how that job interview went or just to chat. My heart has been ripped out, and my chest is filled with salt.

Having to go back to work, remembering how

to do a job I left decades ago, using technology that I can't even remember, working with people whose names I forgot over the years. Letting myself into that old, mouldy flat I lived in back then. Back now. I sometimes find myself absentmindedly driving home. To my real home. But obviously, it's not there. It never was.

My therapist suggested a support group. It's a rare condition, but there are enough people with it to warrant a meeting. I drove for over four hours to be there.

All I wanted was to be in a room where people didn't expect me to remember who they were dating in this one utterly ordinary month in our twenties when all I can see is their face after all of that chemo. It's very difficult hanging out with people you've seen age and die.

The meeting was held at some rented office space. Could have been anywhere. I parked, only a few minutes late. And on one of the chairs, looking nervous, sat my wife.

A Farewell Note

***

Robert Graver

Diary Entry #607 - A Farewell Note.

Hey, it's me again. Are you surprised to see my words still being written? Are you sorry yet? If you're reading this, have you forgiven yourself? I doubt it. You're probably still stuck in your narcissistic ways, treating everyone around you like you are a God given gift to mankind. Pathetic.

By now, as you know if you are reading this, then I am gone. I have finally escaped the stranglehold you placed around my life, my neck most of the time. The nightmare that I was living whilst under your roof has pushed me to pen this final entry.

I hope you're happy. Actually, fuck that. I hope you get hit by a truck, and get dragged under every single wheel, slowly, and *even* then, I hope that doesn't kill you. I hope you survive. I want you to live with the pain of all those broken bones, the bruises, the embarrassment of being seen as such a weak and pathetic excuse of a person.

No, I want you to die with no one around you, alone, in a hospital bed, where even the nurses can't or won't save you. I want you to suffer years of mental torment eating away at your soul for the things you put me through. But as you gulp down the mush from your feeding tube, you choke. Ah, that would put a smile across my face, for the first time in years. Too late for that now, though, right?

For anyone else reading this entry, I hope you have read the rest of my diary. If you haven't, let me catch you all up.

My name is Cassie, and I'm thirty-four - well, I was. Who knows how old I would be now, whenever you are reading this? I thought my life was about to change for the better when I met Craig. He was caring, charming, loveable. The main word there is 'was'. He was all of these things, at least in the beginning when we met.

I was in love. Deeply, and truly in love. I couldn't imagine my life with anyone else apart from Craig. The first few months were great, perfect even. We rushed into life head on with no brakes, no crash helmets. That's something I regret now, though, because my whole world came crashing down after we moved in together.

We had found a nice house, far from perfect, but I saw it as a project. Whilst Craig went off to work in the city, earning enough money for us both to live a comfortable life, I would stay at home. I would clean and fix the place up. Like I said, it needed work, but it was doable.

I remember the day he first came home drunk.

Not the tipsy kind of drunk, but the kind of drunk that changed a person. You could see in his eyes that the man I loved was no longer present. What did I do wrong? I still don't know, but something, somewhere inside his twisted and demented mind, snapped.

That was the first time he hit me. Hard. I mean, yeah, in the bedroom he liked to slap me around a bit, and I enjoyed that. But this. *This* was different. This wasn't consensual: this was anger. Rage. I put it down to jealousy and insecurities within his own mind. I know he had been in bad relationships in the past; being cheated on, being looked down at like a piece of shit. Maybe that was what triggered his first outburst.

As he came through the front door, I was washing the dishes in the kitchen. I heard my phone buzz on the table in the other room, thinking nothing of it. It was probably just Michelle sending me another stupid dog photo on Reddit. This is what tipped him over the edge.

Michelle and I had a weird relationship. We would constantly take the piss out of each other, ridicule the other over stupid things. But neither of us ever took any offense. It was just how our friendship worked.

She was dyslexic, so, of course I had to use this against her whenever I could. The best reminder was that her name in my address book was saved as Michel; how she used to spell her name in elementary school. I can see how a six year old would reach the conclusion that their name was spelt like this - speaking out the phonics of the word, just how she was taught, 'Mich.' 'El.' Michel. If you are reading this, Michelle, I'm sorry. I didn't want to put you through any of the hurt you are no doubt experiencing.

But this message, as it popped up on my phone, sent Craig's insecurities and jealousy on a downward spiral.

"Who the fuck is Michel?!"

He stormed into the kitchen, throwing the phone at me, narrowly missing my head, smashing to pieces against the wall. I didn't even have time to explain the inside joke to him before his hands were around my throat, squeezing the air from my lungs. I clasped at his hands, trying to pry his fingers from my neck. It was no use. Just as I was on the brink of passing out, he let go, slapping my face with the back of his hand, demanding I tell him who this person texting me was. I could barely even draw a breath through my bruised airway, let alone get any words out. He marched back out of the room, slamming every door possible on his way to the garden for a smoke.

I just sat there, weeping, on the floor. Was this my fault? Did I do this to him? I didn't really know how to react to what just happened. I decided the best course of action was to ignore it. Pass it off as a one off, a simple misunderstanding, and too much alcohol in his system.

Boy, was I wrong! The violence continued; the

abuse carried on; the bruises never healed. It was probably a good thing I rarely left the house. Maybe if I had, someone would have noticed. I couldn't really go anywhere. He took the Mustang to work, the closest store was a good two or three kilometres away, and I had a lot of housework to keep on top of.

The turning point of this relationship, when I realised it wasn't my fault, was when he tried to make it all about him. Like I said, he was narcissistic, the dog's bollocks. Everything needed to be about him.

I should have seen the signs, read the clues. But I didn't, because I was blinded by my overwhelming love for the man I thought was the one. For two years I let him abuse me and use me. Hit me. Choke me. Throw things at me. Rape me. I just couldn't see a way out of it.

The night he threw a bowl of soup at me was the worst. It smashed against my shoulder, sending the scalding liquid all over my face and arms, the bowl shattering into pieces. It wasn't 'flavourful' enough he told me. As I lay on the floor, screaming in pain, he picked up one of the broken shards and held it to his wrists, threatening to cut himself. This was how twisted his head was.

He did it as well. He slit his wrists because it didn't taste good enough. My cooking was inadequate. It wasn't about me this time. In this fucked up head of his, he concluded that I didn't love him, because I made his soup taste like shit.

This was justifiable enough to inflict abuse upon himself, just because he thought I didn't love him. He was willing to hurt, even kill, himself just over a thought of my love not being as strong enough towards him as his love was to me.

Fucking nutcase, right?

The paramedics came, passing off the situation as an attempted suicide. The balls this guy had to tell the doctors that it was MY fault! MY FAULT that he had attempted to take his own life! I mean, what the actual fuck?

Like, really. The paramedics didn't even notice any signs of my struggle, of my abuse. He had forced me to wear a long sleeved cardigan to cover the bruises. He turned the heating off, making the house as cold as possible, forcing me to wear a scarf to cover the marks on my neck. He wasn't dumb. He had logic. Everything he did to me was calculated. He knew how to hide any evidence of me being the victim. This was when I knew there was only one way out. I couldn't live with this, this monster. Not anymore. I had put up with his shit for long enough.

One night when he was sleeping, I crept out of the bedroom and began to write this entry. How I managed to keep my diary hidden from him for so long, I still don't know. Maybe he wasn't as smart as I thought. I hid it in places he would never look, like the laundry basket. When did he ever take the opportunity to help me with household chores?

That was my job. Never his.

Either way, if he had ever found this, no doubt I would be long dead before getting this far into my journal. Every account, every time he has hit me, hurt me, done anything to me, is all accounted for in this book. I hope he reads it all. I hope the police read it all. I hope it sends him away for a long time.

The night I left him alone in bed, was the last time I saw his face. It looked peaceful. It looked like the man I had fallen in love with. I sneaked out of the house as quietly as I could, and if you are reading this, then I know my work is done. My journal has reached the public eye. I posted the book through the letterbox of 1124 Franklin Crescent. A charming doctor, Pete, lived there. I knew that he would be able to get my account seen, get it heard.

I haven't actually done the deed as I pen these details. But if you are reading this, then it worked. I know this is how it is going to go. Craig will wake up in the morning, go into the bathroom for a piss, and miss the bowl, inevitably, as I always have to clean up his lousy aim. He'll find me in the bathtub, my wrists torn open, a razor blade on the edge of the tub. I will leave a final note beside my lifeless body.

"Don't be sorry for taking my life. Be sorry for making me live it."

Part Six: Artifices and Realties

What is Reality?

A question to answer;
The answer lays bare,
All questions of what
Makes man question there

Are we doomed to forsake
All our gifts to ourselves?
Are we forever to question,
Our own love, or our hell?

Remove all the masks
And what do you see?
Hard wires, and plastic,
Or a soul that is free?

- S. Nicolas

ID - entities

***

Maria Claudia Bada

'The spectacle is not a collection of images; it is a social relation between people that is mediated by images' (Guy Debord, Society of the spectacles)
Spammers.

I remember when I was deleting identities without regrets. Just a few doubts - I can easily sort them out. Moderating a community is a real job, indeed. Every day, nine to five, I surf amidst a virtual sea of spam, catch the bad guys, and obliterate them. Game over, folks.

Just three - four steps, in a precise, swift procedure and my own judgment separate their bully and daring virtual ID from a certain death.

I love my job. I am one of those pulp-fiction space captains on a solo trip - trying to float with a small control mouse and airbook ship in the centre of the overflowing spamming maelstrom. Some days, the shining light of great content is swallowed by distant black holes in a galaxy made of deal making filibusters and selfies' cultists.

First rule of a good moderator: don't trust any user too much.

It's a mine-field down there in the forums. You gotta watch out. You've got to watch each other's backs with your faithful teammates.

The hours got diluted in a series of infinite mortal loops, swallowing not-too-fancy interior designers, solicitors from remote angles of the globe, international electronic cigarettes, and the best travel agencies in the world. Not always does the captain win and get the girl in this storyline. The forbidden forest of expletives in so many languages is disclosing its treasures to the eager net-sailors. You also get bombarded from your allies, here. Your best friend reporting spam and abuse can be the most heartbreaking. A traitor stabbing you rudely in the back using the same techniques and inappropriate language you thought only spammers and trolls are capable of.

If historians could look in ten, fifty, a hundred years at all the debris of this spammy ocean made of millions of electronics pollution produced by our users, they would have a true glimpse into our era - it is not a case you got climate changes and looming disasters ahead.

Second rule of a good moderator: law and order exist

Rules can lead you in most cases and have a precise URL to spread around the Verb to newbies, in particular.

There is always a written rule for you to follow. The second you sign up and decide to follow all these enthusiastic white sheep and enter a virtual forum to share your experience, you abide. It is a no-coming back situation. If you are in, you need to behave. But the black sheep in you awakes the very second you click "enter the forum". This hidden monster starts pushing the borders of the netiquette, conquering a new level of indecency and finally gets you. A flicker in your eyes mirrored back by the screen betrays your inner bad self. That mouth-filth, angry, troll persona is blossoming, nurtured by your keyboards.

You are discovering your ugliest side, inside the blanket of your profile's name. It's fast and exciting. A figment of pleasure rises in you and moves both your hands. What the hell are you typing? Well, yeah, you are violating the rules. You are now on the wild side and you are posting, posting, posting endlessly, counting the hours before you get caught. Inevitably the black sheep can't survive - apologies, but we are not Samaritans. We don't want to forcibly convert you to our cult. We don't need to.

Third rule of a good moderator: please do not become an online mass murderer - be kind and understanding.

Don't ask me who is watching the watcher. This is my job and I do it sensibly. Before virtually ending anyone, I ponder over and over again.

I will never say something like, "As a reminder, please can you stop being a perfectly functioning Jekyll in the real world, who uses the keyboard as a weapon of virtual disruptive behaviour?"

The fact that you are bored, sad, and miserable doesn't find any place here. Promoting your own business, is none of our business.

We have the supremacy made of moral

decency and law enforcement. But we are fair and just, without being priests or policemen. The execrable passions you exhibit in other virtual bars, all the hidden desires and depravities you wish to advertise have no haven here.

Maybe we are angels? So, please, say your prayers quickly and relinquish your user's ID to a superior ruler.

The virus of bad behaviour is spreading like a mortal bug. Can you stop being a bloody virtual Hyde please? It is beautiful to be normal, for once. Maybe you are not used to thinking hard, and in fact if you still didn't have this habit, thinking whatsoever is a highly discouraged practice for you. You are going to be terminated on-line for that precise reason.

Maybe I am an undertaker. The kind you find in the cowboy movies. I don't care if you are a good or bad fella, you are getting down here in my ol' town and want to fight in front of my citizens. You want to trash my streets and take my women, terrorising everyone. I am taking the measurements for your coffin.

No Armageddon for you. No purgatory. I am the judge and the jury, a sheriff with all stripes and stars shining in the unforgettable sun, waiting for your gun to fire hate speech, commercial idiosyncratic ads, obscenity. Are you kissing your ol' mom with that mouth, mate? Two more clicks, and you won't be a virtual being anymore. Bang-bang. Discharged. Done and dusted.

Maybe I am a little god of such a small,

personal nicknamed cosmos. Deleting entities through their funny ID. No one got injured in the process, no worries. We always play by the rules. You can create a new spammy email and enroll again with the same intentions but, as a reminder, you're gonna die again and again and again, like a never-ending video-game.

Watch your back...

Marginal Creatures

***

Theresa Williams

We are the things that live at the edges, in the margins. We are scavengers, content to live freely, beholden to no one. We take only the things that no one else wants. We are invisible or almost nearly so. We are that half-forgotten after-image of bright sunlight, the negative. Dust motes. Shimmers on water. Reflections. Shadows. And this is my story.

I am the margins on this page. White space. Empty space. Or is it? Do you see a shape moving along the edges? My face is being formed while the author types. Where are my eyes? Do I have eyes? Do I have a nose? A mouth? Or is the text typed on this page like a null mask? And, if it is a null mask, what is being hidden?

I am hiding from you, my dear. I say "my" dear, but you are not mine at all, are you? I am yours though. Cover me! My original message is hidden, that lemon water script is all but gone, save you hold me close to a flame. But, don't do that! Else, I will burn. But cover me! Cover me with ink. For I am thine and I exist to be negated.

We are the whole things. The solid things made of matter. Flat enough to write on have you quill, pen or computer to do the scribing. We exist to provide balance. Heaviness. Weight that you can rely upon. We are big and bold, unafraid to say that we are here. Without us, there would be no shadows, no margins, no edges. Those words would have no meaning. We are the land, the sea, the sky upon which all things dwell and write out their lives.

We are the words, the ink, the digital text. Without us, there would be no message. You both would live pointless lives. There would be no communication, no contract, no wedding vows. While we don't make the matter, we provide the limits. We create the margins, the edges, the spaces. We are your GOD.

The little girl entered the room carrying a red marker. She found the piece of paper and used her red crayon to color the paper.

Sometime later, the father came in carrying a string with the cat trailing behind him. Seeing the paper, he crumpled the paper and tied the string around it. The cat followed him, batting playfully at the crumpled paper.

The white space, paper and ink paused their arguing for a moment.

"I'm still the most important," said the white space.

"No! I am the most important," said the ink. The crayon echoed his words.

"It is perfectly obvious that I am the most important," said the paper. "Without me, there would be no cat toy."

The white space and ink looked at each other. "That's not true," they began. The argument continued down the hall as the father and the cat left the house.

The Pigeon

***

Ann Powell Lewis

I stopped for a minute and did a mental check of my body. I don't feel pain anywhere. Maybe the voodoo hasn't kicked in yet if someone is actually sticking pins in a doll that looks like me.

Mario looked concerned. "Two days in a row? Are you having a love affair with someone else's man?"

"Good grief, Mario, of course I'm not! I'm 64 years old with two ex-husbands. I have no interest in dealing with men at this point in my life."

That's not 100% true. I do have a Tinder profile, but that's mainly for entertainment. I've only been on one actual Tinder date and it was so dreadful that I doubt if I'll ever go on another one.

Mario looked at me suspiciously. "Are you certain? Because the number one thing that voodoo is used for is to get revenge on a cheating spouse or lover. There are no men you have contact with?"

"Well, of course I have contact with men. I'm sitting here with you right now, and even though you're young enough to be my son—"

"Grandson," Mario corrected.

I sighed. "Okay, grandson. I also see the one-armed butcher at least twice a week to buy meat for my dogs, and then there are the male cashiers at the grocery store; basically, I see men every day. Are their wives and girlfriends going to try to kill me? I honestly don't think I pose much of a threat."

Ha. That's an understatement. I've let myself go since I retired in Mexico. I never go to the salon to cut my long gray hair anymore—why bother? I just pull it back in a ponytail. I'm a few pounds heavier than I should be, what with all the chips and margaritas. And I don't even own any makeup. Who would I put it on for? My dogs? My life is as perfect as it's ever been. I eat, sleep, walk the dogs, practice my Spanish and putter around the garden.

The garden! I suddenly remember Jesus, the elderly gardener who came with my apartment. And his elderly wife who lives with him in the tiny casita in one corner of the hacienda's garden.

"Oh my god, Mario! I just remembered something," I said.

"What?" Now Mario was the one leaning forward, eager for details.

"There's this ancient gardener, Jesus, who came with my apartment. He doesn't do much actual gardening, and I swear he must be 100 years old—but he has a wife."

"Ah," said Mario. "And this ancient gardener, does he talk to you? Flirt with you?"

"Kind of," I said. "I guess. But I never thought much of it, because—well, he's so old. And I know I'm old too, and look ancient to

175

someone as young as you, but Jesus is in a different category of old. Plus, he's missing most of his teeth. Maybe all of them—I never wanted to look too closely."

Mario nodded as if he now understood why the black pigeon was haunting me.

"If I were you, I would move out of that apartment before it's too late. If the bird is there for 7 days in a row, I'm afraid you are doomed."

"Doomed? What do you mean?" I was feeling panicky and ridiculous at the same time.

"I think you know the definition of 'doomed'," Mario said. "Thank you for the beers. I hope to see you again." He pushed his chair back from the table and departed. It was almost like he was afraid he'd catch my 'doomed'-ness if he hung around any longer.

Anyway, that was yesterday when I last saw Mario. Now, this morning, the black pigeon is there again. Day number 3. As I watch him looking through the glass with one evil little yellow eye, I feel a sudden pain just behind my belly button. I press on it, hard, with the palm of one hand, and the pain subsides. I yank the curtains closed so I can't see the bird and drag out my suitcase from underneath the bed. I have no intention of staying here for 7 days of bird sightings. The dogs and I can check into a pet-friendly hotel I know just off the Jardin de las Ranas, and I'll ask the landlord to ship over the rest of my few belongings. She can keep my security deposit. Another stab of pain shoots through, deeper in my abdomen this time. I start throwing clothes into the suitcase.

Savage Eyes

***

Thomas Govaers

Amelia is wandering the streets as a red sun dawns on the city that already feels cold. She doesn't feel the cold anymore, watching the steam vent out of the chimneys and outlets, breathing life into the city. The rhythmic clinging of her brass feet is in line with the clanking and whistling of distant factories.

There aren't many people outside: they're probably all working in the factories or hidden if they refuse to work. Why won't some of them just work? That's their purpose, right? Amelia glances inside an alleyway - that's where the pauper savages are hidden. That's where they live, like the vermin they are. The cockroaches! They've lost all their humanity by choosing to live in the dirt. Were they ever human at all? They don't grow in quality of life at all, just in quantity. They die because they won't learn. They crawl over each other in that little alleyway. Wasteful lives! Amelia only looks for a fraction of a second, but amidst this scene of poor people minding their own business, there is a face looking straight at Amelia. It's the face of a little girl. The face is stained with dirt and coal, but the eyes are so clean and innocent.

This image of the little girl looking at her seems to be burned on her mind. What did the girl expect of her? Amelia can't shake it off or just ignore it. Why not? She has forgotten so many things she can't really feel anymore, and still, there is a weird sensation in her chest. Her brass arms seem heavier than they already are. The image of the eyes takes her back to her youth, to her father's tearoom. It had a colossal mirror on one side. She saw a little human girl in that mirror, with a beautiful dress and bright eyes, staring back at her. Her father summoned her for evening tea. It was the only moment of the week she was allowed to talk to her father, instead of just talking to the maid or Mr. Douglas, her tutor.

"Father, why don't I have to work in the factory?"

"Why would a beautiful and clever girl like you want to do that?"

"Wouldn't it be fair?"

"Oh, little Amelia, but it is fair!"

"How so?"

"Well, we have our own business cut out for us."

"When do I have to work then?"

"Oh, well, right now you have to study all kinds of languages like Latin and French, and mathematics. You like studying, right?"

"I do, but sometimes it's boring."

"So, that's your work right now, to prepare yourself for the future to come."

This answer sounded logical for now and she thought about it. Why didn't it feel right?

"But, it still seems a bit different. Why don't

they have to study?"

"Ha! Don't let the people in the factories hear your childish contemplations - they would go on strike! And society would go back hundreds of years. No, darling, we are advanced humans. We see that everyone has their purpose and qualities. They, the savages, aren't really built to do the thinking. Everything would fall back into chaos. Just like we aren't born to work in a factory - imagine me doing all that manual labour. It would get my three-piece suit dirty! And all my potential would be wasted."

"Why us?"

"Oh Amelia, you're so bright, but you're still like an uncut piece of glass. Pay attention with Mr. Douglas; he will shape you, so you will be formed like a neat monocle, you see? But for now, I'll just tell you we were given this machine because we are advanced. We outgrew the savage humanity. We're the future."

Amelia's father was right: what strange questions she used to ask as a child. But seeing the girl has woken something inside her. What was it she saw in those eyes? It was something she only remembers from childhood - from a time before the accident happened and they had to revive her as a hybrid. She doesn't remember the accident itself: that memory got wiped, so she didn't have to experience the trauma again. Trauma is something that clouds the mind. She does remember the pain though - how it felt; strange that she should remember the sensation when now she can't feel pain anymore. It was a painful process, becoming a hybrid: the pain ebbed away slowly, and the numbness took over.

Walking back to her mansion, she starts shaking off the feeling. "The whole reason I'm alive is because I adapt," she thinks out loud. "That makes me stronger and more fit than other humans."

She reaches her metal door and, in the reflection, she sees her own eyes looking back at her.

Turing Test Game Show

***

Theresa Williams

"It's like the date I've always wanted. It's like 8 solid hours of sleep in one night. It's like that feeling when you first fall in love."

"It's good, then, huh?"

"Yeah." Leah paused. "Your turn."

"You want me to describe the taste of the ice cream?"

"Yeah." She shoved the cup of ice cream through the slot to the other person.

Grasslee made a fair amount of noise getting the ice cream. He clanked the spoon against the bowl. He smacked his lips. "Uuhhhuumm." He drew the word out till it had 4 syllables.

"It tastes like pistachio."

"It is pistachio."

"It tastes like pistachio if it was the richest, most handsome dude in the world."

"Not a girl?"

Grasslee smacked his lips again. "Yep. Yep. Yep. No, definitely a guy. Not a girl."

"It's really sweet!"

"Not a girl."

"Smooth. Creamy."

"Those are guy characteristics. If this ice cream were a man, it would be a gigolo, or a movie star. Yeah, definitely a movie star."

182

"Clark Gable?"

"This century! Chris Hemsworth. Yeah, bold, muscular, creamy and rich."

"Alrighty then," the MC announced to the audience. "Welcome back to the Turing Test. Our three contestants have just listened to an interaction between a computer and a human. Their job is to figure out which one is which. The winner(s) will receive one million dollars. Each person will announce their choice and their reason why. At the end, each contestant will have one more opportunity to change their minds."

He turned to contestant #1. "Alice, as a librarian, you must be good at tracking down information. Which one do you choose?"

"Well, Ryan," she began in somewhat quavering tones. "At first, I thought it must be Grasslee who was the computer, but he smacked his lip, made "um" into a 4-syllable sound and dropped his spoon. So, I am going with Leah. Leah is the computer."

"So, Alice has chosen Leah as the computer. What about Walter, here? Walter, as an accountant, you are used to adding things up. What's your decision?"

"At first," Walter turned towards Alice, "I agreed that it must be Leah for the same reasons Alice stated. But then, I wondered, what if all that stuff Grasslee did was staged to make it look like he was human? It seemed like too much, so I am going to say Grasslee was the computer."

"Ok, so we have 1 for Leah and 1 for Grasslee. Barbara, what say you?"

Barbara twirled her long hair around her finger and stared up at the ceiling. "Normally," she said, "I'm really good at sizing people up. A waitress has to be able to read people. I think I will say that Grasslee is the computer. All of Leah's statements were comparing the ice cream to real human experiences. I don't think a computer would get that."

The MC turned to face the audience again. "There you have it, folks. What do you think? The audience erupted into a cacophony of voices arguing over who each thought was the computer.

He turned to the contestants once more. "Here is your last chance to change your mind. Alice?"

Alice shook her head no.

"Walter?"

Walter looked upset, like he might cry. He put a fist up to his lips, muffled a yelp and replied, "No. I am staying."

"Barbara?"

"I agree with Alice that what Grasslee did seemed a bit over the top. But I also agree with Walter that that could all have been staged."

"So, you've decided?"

Her face got noticeably quiet. "I'm sticking with Grasslee. He's the computer."

The house band began their drumroll. The MC announced, "and the winner is…" He opened the envelope and stood, looking puzzled. Seeming to catch himself, he said, "Will the human come on out?"

A beautiful black-haired woman walked out on stage, followed by a handsome blonde-haired man.

"Wait!?" Alice and Walter called at the same time.

"They're both human," Barbara cried.

"Yes," the MC said. "It seems the producers pulled a fast one on us. Neither Leah nor Grasslee is the computer."

"There's no computer?"

"No. There's a computer all right. It's me. I didn't know myself until I read the note. I am the computer! I won the Turing Test!"

Part Seven: 24 Twenty-Four Word Stories

Twenty Four, Never More

You challenge me this,
You challenge me that,
You want me to fall off a cliff
And go SPLAT?

You want me to lie down
And wait for the Sun?
You want me to wait
For a love that will come?

...

So, what is your challenge?
You want me to compose
A whole story in
Two dozen words, I suppose!

- S. Nicolas

24 Twenty-Four Word Stories

One day, he decided to get milk. He picked the cutest cashier for checkout when she asked: "Have you found everything you're looking for?"

- Thomas Govaers

One day, the dead rose from their graves, zombies stalked the streets and Jessica discovered that she had chipped one of her expensive nails.

- Jane Andrews

One day, after many months of darkness, the sun came out, flowers bloomed, and the birds chirped. Humans, you asked? No longer a tellurian .

- Renee Schnebelin

One day, the black dog waived his tail. The man behind the glass smiled at him and said: "you have a new home, buddy."

- Anne-Charlotte Gerbaud

Big eyes. Tiny fingers holding onto my sister.

Old door repainted to welcome you.

Two bodies. "This is a special one."

Door opens.

You.

- Beth Collins

One day, after you die, you will still feel everything. I should be flattered; my husband still finds me attractive after all these years.

- Robert Graver

"One day this will all be yours, darling."
BANG!
"Who wants to wait for some day?" I said. "When I can have it now?"

- Theresa Williams

I was on the cliffs that day, and I had a story to finish about us. I find endings so difficult. She ended it.

- John Harper

One day, two proto-chickens met up and had a good time. Later, the first egg appeared and inadvertently sparked the longest debate ever held.

- Samia Nicolas

One day, an incompetent university lecturer attended his professor's house party, insulted the guests, and set fire to a bed. Not so lucky, Jim.

- Jane Andrews

One day the world will sing again, but for now I will just lie on the ground, waiting for Jesus. Look! There he is!

- Theresa Williams

One day, Alexia awoke to a chaotic scene in Del Plazo. Smoke filled streets; Littles screamed; Aardsmen filled streets. Boom! Then there was silence.

- Renee Schnebelin

One day, after all those years, he decided to speak to her. She smiled, looked at him, and said "I've been waiting for you."

- Anne-Charlotte Gerbaud

One day, the chosen one will forget to fulfill his destiny, and all of fate rests on your shoulders, instead. You save the universe.

- Samia Nicolas

I was absolutely devastated when my beautiful niece was chosen as this year's harvest's virgin sacrifice to the Gods.
I've fucking doomed us all.

- Robert Graver

One day, all the good guys die, and the bad guys win. Then the bad guys are usurped by worse guys. The cycle continues.

- Samia Nicolas

A noise came from the living room. I swept my flashlight over the cabinet of porcelain dolls. I watched in horror. Their pupils contracted.

- Robert Graver

One day, a rabbit made an acquaintance with a daffodil. They chatted every day for two weeks. Afterwards the rabbit said goodbye to his friend.

- Samia Nicolas

They felt they had tamed nature.
Though, now rain falls, they run, hiding inside, tamed by the nature they used to be part of.

- Thomas Govaers

Marriage: It's your turn to clean the litter box, my wife said. The cat watched me scoop his shit. He's not even my cat.

- Ann Powell Lewis

One day being and existing will coincide into a moment of fullness - a one-way ticket journey, but I really want to take this train.

- Maria Claudia Bada

"One day, I'll be older than you," said my little sister.
"But you'll never be faster than me," I replied, grabbing her snickerdoodle cookie.

- Theresa Williams

You have a weird habit of running up the stairs after turning off the lights.
Do you think I'd wait for a silly light?

- Robert Graver

Today, Feria the Great Purple Elephant awoke with great ambitions. She wanted to sail a boat. Could she do it? ... Of course she could!

- Renee Schnebelin

Part Eight: Anything Goes

Heartbreaker

Without love I am so lonely and sad.
Two days ago, she left me. Just friends?
Friend's? We can never be that. So, freaking mad!
Stupid!

She had to know how this would end.
You shouldn't be so angry, she said.
Angry? I shouted as I grabbed her head.
Please, no. She cried, writhed, and screamed.

I squeezed tighter until her heart stopped beating.
What have I done? Oh, no. Her body, limp.
He will come looking for her soon. Think, quick!
I grab a sheet and rolled her in. So heavy, wimp.
Ugh, where should I hide her body? The crick!

Out the back window she fell with a thud.
Into the crick and then sank in the mud.

- R. Schnebelin

We Are All Born Colour Blind

***

Samia Nicolas

I have a superpower. No, it's not being able to fly, or the ability to turn invisible. Though sometimes I wish that was my super power. Turning invisible, I mean. My super power is simple. I can't stand by. I can't leave it be. I can't let something unfair happen to someone and do nothing about it. Why is it a super power? Well, aren't super powers meant to be something extraordinary? Something no one else has the power to do? That's how it seemed that day: the day I realised I was different to everyone else.

I was on the train back home after a drama rehearsal at school; my A-level assessed performance was coming up and we were in trouble. The carriage was packed with people coming home from work, I guess. I was minding my own business, like pretty much everyone else. Same as every day. Except today there had been some sporting thing on in the city: someone had won a cup or medal or whatever, and there had been a parade. The train was packed more than usual, and you could spot the fans, and not just because they were all wearing the same colours; most of them were, as my mum puts it, "merry". Drunk, as my dad would say.

So us regulars, the ones going home from

school and work, were sat doing what we normally do, that great British tradition of being physically, intimately close to someone but pretending you were on your own personal desert island and all you had was a book or headphones or probably both. That was me, anyway. I can't even remember what I was listening to, or even what I was reading. I'm not even sure the music was that quiet because when I realised something was happening, what got my super power senses tingling, I guess, wasn't because I'd heard it. There was this strange, thick feeling in the carriage, like the space had suddenly halved in size. I gave a fleeting look at the people who sat immediately near me. I was fairly sure they had sensed it too. Guy with Glasses turned slightly towards the window; Too Much Make-up Lady pressed the volume button on her phone; Grumpy Face started putting her headphones in; Weed Man (stature, not drug preference) bent further into his book. I couldn't get a good look at Pretty Lady — she sat on the other side of Grumpy Face in my row, but I knew she was there because I had seen her get on the stop after mine, and recognised her as a true regular. Then I realised a large man standing in the aisle was talking to her. I took my headphones out.

He was one of the fan boys, though I guess 'boy' wasn't really a good description. He wasn't even dressed completely in the kit - just a token coloured shirt with the name of the team on it. He was tall, beefy, and white. Though that last word was a stretch as he was more beetroot in colour.

One chunky arm hung languidly off a handlebar from the ceiling, and he had a sneer on his lips as he spoke. It took me a little while to figure out what he was saying, but I put that down to incredulity rather than his lack of elocution (Miss Adjobe says I'm getting an A* in English). He was certainly loud enough for everyone in the carriage to hear.

'Why don't you take that thing off? It's hot in here. You must be boiling in that thing.'

I leaned forward a little to see that Pretty Lady wasn't looking at him. I also noticed Fan Man's eyes flicker toward me, then back at Pretty Lady.

'Come on, Paki, what's the matter? Can't answer a question? I'm trying to find out about your culture.' He laughed when he said it. 'Why don't you take it off? I'm asking nicely.'

I looked around to see if anyone else was seeing and hearing the same as me. My fellow seated commuters were, if anything, even more insular, shrinking themselves into oblivion. The others standing in the aisle, pretty much next to Fan Man, were all turned away. Behind Fan Man were more fan boys, maybe his friends, but I could see they were actually trying to squeeze further away from him into the crowded space by the doors – not very successfully either. Fan Man was the opposite of a black hole.

'What have you got to hide, huh? Lemme guess – you, er, haven't washed your hair, ever! How do you wash your hair anyway if you never take it off? Do you shower with it? Hey, do you fuck with that thing on?'

197

I heard a few tuts. Anonymous tuts.

I felt something inside my belly. It was hot, and it was rising.

He was chuckling to himself now, a sickly shine to his eyes. 'Were you born with it on? Of course not! So why the fuck do you have to wear one, huh? For Allah? But if you weren't born with it, then he's already damned you right. Fucking idiots.'

The heat grew to my chest, my shoulders. I looked around at the adults in the carriage again, trying to catch their eyes, urging them to do or say something. I heard a few more tuts.

'I know, I know, it's to keep spare curry under there. I bet if I pulled it off, there'd be a tikka masala under it, ha ha ha!'

I couldn't take it anymore.

'Excuse me – you're being rude.'

Funny thing about super powers. They make an impact when you use them. The air seemed to hold its breath. Even though everyone was turned away, I felt like all the eyes were pointed directly at me. Including Fan Man's.

He looked me up and down, which didn't take long; I'm only five foot three. I said I had a super power, not a superhero physique.

He laughed. Then turned back to the lady.

'You don't like what I'm saying? Then go back to whatever foreign country you came from, Paki.'

I stood up. 'Hey, you have no right to say anything to her. Leave her alone.'

'I have no right?' Fan Man turned back to me;

I had his full attention now. 'This is my country, not hers. She should fuck off home.'

'She *is* home: this is her country as much as yours. And she doesn't need some white guy telling her what she can and can't wear, or where to go.'

The air was taut like an elastic band on a hand sling. I was shaking, but not with fear.

'My dad didn't fight in the Gulf so that these Pakis could come and take my jobs. And if they're going to wear towels on their heads, then they gotta take them off because this is England!'

'That was a long sentence. Did you remember to breathe?'

'Listen, mate, I don't have beef with you. You're all right, you're English.' He actually tried to dismiss me with a charming smile.

'Yeah, that's right, I'm English. But you do have a beef with me, because as long as you insult this lady here, you're insulting me too. You're insulting my country by being a racist dick.'

The air coiled; the oxygen seemed to leave the carriage. Fan Man's face got redder, and for a short moment I genuinely believed there really was no oxygen and he was suffocating. But no, I had just hit a button.

'You little bitch,' he spat. 'You don't fucking say that to me!'

'Oh, don't like it so much now? So, it was okay when you were insulting the lady, but not okay when someone insults you, you utter wanker?'

'She's a fucking Paki!' Like that excused everything. 'Go on, you're probably not really

English, right. Go on and fuck her then you love her so much.'

'What is it? Does it make you happy picking on women smaller than you? Is that what makes you feel like a real man? Well guess what, you're nothing but a spineless prick. Apologise to her. Apologise to her.'

The tension finally gave, like a gust of coastal air flying through. Through my rage, I began to hear something that I slowly realised had been in the background for a little while. Voices. Joining me. I looked around. More than one person was filming with their phone. Everyone was looking. Engaged and looking.

'Leave them alone.'
'You go home!'
'Get sober and sod off.'
'We don't agree with you. Go away.'
'Ignore this guy. He's nothing.'

'Fuck off, all of you, to Pakiland!' Fan Man backed into the space between the doors where now space had miraculously been made. Then I realised the train had stopped, and the guy was getting off. People started to clap sarcastically as the doors closed; they started to cheer and jeer at him as he stood there on the platform – a lonely station by the look of it. At least his friends were still on the train, further down the carriage now, heads ducked. I figured this wasn't his stop.

And then it was almost normal. People cleared

their throats; phone calls were made and the incident recited. People made eye contact, with each other and me, nodding proudly. But the Lady was sitting there, looking into her lap. I leaned over to her. Grumpy Face made some room.

'Hey, I... I'm really sorry about that.'

She looked up at me, eyes glistening. 'It's okay. I... thank you. You didn't have to do that.'

'I feel so awful for you. Are you... okay?'

She smiled and gave a nervous laugh, her finger flicking the corner of one eye. Then she frowned and shook her head.

'Where are you from?' I said, then suddenly realised what that could have meant. 'I mean, what stop, not... you know.'

'Uh... I get off at the next stop. It's okay, I know what you meant. You're right, I am British. Third generation. My grandparents are from Nigeria.'

'Well, I don't get off until after that, so... you have someone at home?'

She nodded. 'My sister.'

'Good, I'm glad you have someone to talk to. I'm just really sorry you had to go through that.'

'It... it's not unusual. I'm used to it.'

I thought my blood had cooled, but this brought it right back up to temperature.

'That's not right.'

'No. But it's life. This is my stop.' She stood up awkwardly as I was in her way. We shuffled around each other and she made her way to the door. 'Thanks for saying something.'

Then she was gone.

I never saw her on the train again.

And I never backed down from anything like that from then on. Why do some people act that way when they are confronted with someone of a different race, or religion, or whatever? Pretty Lady had dark brown skin. But that's not what I noticed about her first. In fact, I didn't notice until Fan Man had started his whole thing. If I thought about all the regulars, I probably couldn't tell you what skin colour they all were. I learned in Health and Social Care that everyone is born colour blind. That's really, really true. To think that someone with different skin to you is somehow less than you are is something you learn, not something you're born with. My mum said that most people weren't like that. Most people were good.

I know I'm not the only one with this super power. But if what my mum said is true, why aren't there more?

'Good' Dog

***

Ann Powell Lewis

August 2015

I think I'm a good dog. I truly do. Of course, I don't really have much to compare myself to because my family isn't one for the dog park or for lingering to chat with fellow dog walkers during my daily morning constitutional. The point being that I don't converse with other dogs, don't discuss the moral ins and outs of what is expected and/or required of those of us holding the position of 'family dog'. There was Teddy, the miniature poodle who resided in our home for just under 3 years until he met an untimely demise while chasing the neighbor's escaped pet rabbit ('BunBun') into the path of an oncoming panel truck. But I don't really count Teddy the poodle as the voice of anything that could possibly be enlightening as far as expectations of canine behavior go. Teddy had a brain the size of a ridiculously small peanut. His days were spent yapping frantically at passers-by he observed on the sidewalk outside our urban

Craftsman cottage in Berkeley, California. He suffered from severe separation anxiety as well and cried continuously when he could not be sitting next to Sunny, sitting on her if at all possible. I have more dignity and self-control in one toenail than Teddy could ever have hoped to possess.

My earliest memory of my life begins three years ago in a chain link kennel at the Berkeley Animal Shelter. I was somewhere between six and eight months old - at least that's what the sign said outside my kennel. I'm not sure where I lived prior to the shelter, but it's not pertinent to this story anyway. The shelter was an unnerving place to be: constant yapping from stressed animals, the odor of fear permeating the atmosphere, and that sinister room in the back that dogs were seen entering but never exiting. Whenever a potential adopter walked through the big sliding glass doors at the front entrance, all the dogs immediately began barking and jumping up and down at the front of their kennels, trying to attract the human's attention. "Me, pick me, please, please, please, pick me!"

I wanted to be adopted too, naturally, but being of superior intelligence (I'm a mixed breed, but predominantly German Shepherd, confirmed by a DNA test recently done by my adoptive family, so my intelligence is markedly greater than that of the average dog), I observed that the humans frequently seemed to be intimidated by the hyperactivity of my fellow canines, particularly if the dogs were large in size, and many of them were. It's not fair, but the fact of the matter is that small dogs are more likely to be adopted, I'm not sure why. Maybe because they eat less, take up less space, and are possibly perceived as cuter (debatable) and easier to drag along on a leash than a pit bull the size of a small car.

I decided that my best bet was to do the opposite of what the other dogs were doing. Instead of barking and jumping all over the place like an idiot, I sat at the door to my kennel, cool as a cucumber and silent. I was careful to make eye contact and smile (yes, I can smile) whenever someone paused by my kennel. If they stuck a finger through the chain links, I didn't lick it because I had also observed that adults do not like getting dog saliva on their hands. (Kids don't mind at all.) What I did was press my snout gently against their fingers as if to say, "Here I am, a highly intelligent, calm, respectful canine. You will not find a better dog to adopt than me. Not here, not anywhere."

And it worked, my technique totally worked. Of course, the first two families that adopted me returned me to the kennel for ridiculous reasons. Perhaps they hadn't realized exactly how much responsibility a dog is, even though I made few demands: food, access to outdoors to relieve myself - really, just the basics. One of the families gave the pathetic excuse for my return as being unable to deal with the hair I shed! I'm a German Shepherd—they could see my magnificent coat in all its long haired glory before they filled out the paperwork and took me home. But humans can be illogical and ridiculous. In fact, I believe that is their natural default state. But the third family that adopted me was the one. They were keepers. The best family ever.

They arrived at the shelter together, one bright Saturday morning, the father, the mother and the three children. Once they saw me and my calm demeanor, the other dogs didn't stand a chance. Well, to be perfectly honest, one of the children, the middle one, Sunny, had her heart set on a brain-dead little brown terrier two kennels down, and wasn't 100% behind the choice of me, but she was outvoted, four to one. I remember the conversation quite clearly.

"Look at this one, Marjoree," the husband

said to his wife. "With all the burglaries in the neighbourhood lately, this one would be a definite deterrent!" He eyed my size and my well-muscled body. I eyed him back. He was fairly large and well-muscled himself. We'd make a good pair.

"But he's—so big," Marjoree replied. "And this sign says he's only six-eight months old. Don't dogs keep growing until about one year old?"

"That's the idea, Babe. A pet chihuahua is certainly not going to deter any would-be criminals." The husband (his name was Bill) stuck his fingers through the chain link and I made my signature, snout-pressing move.

"He does seem nice and calm, which I like," Marjoree said, thoughtfully. "Kids, what do you think of this dog?" All three kids were running up and down the aisles, agitating the dogs. Kelsey, the oldest child, ten at the time, and Sammy, the youngest, aged six, skipped over. Sunny, age eight, stubbornly remained parked beside the terrier.

"He's as big as a pony! Can I ride him to school?" asked Sammy. I said nothing, but I thought to myself that I wouldn't mind giving him a ride to school as long as he didn't grow any heavier. He was a solid looking child and I could tell by the way he was wiggling around and clutching himself that a trip to the toilets was in order.

"Can he sleep with me?" asked Kelsey. She was old enough to be aware of all the talk about crime in the neighborhood; in fact, her best friend Mia, who lived only one street over, had recently had an armed home invasion at her house. Nobody was hurt, but the two thieves stole their televisions and computers, and the entire family had been traumatized by the experience. Kelsey was terrified of the possibility that it could happen at their house, and Mia would not stop talking about it. I was fine with the idea of sleeping with Kelsey. A real bed would be like a fantasy come true after the cold concrete floor of the shelter.

"Sunny, come look at the dog," Marjoree called.

"I want this one," Sunny said. "This one already likes me. I don't want that one."

She was sitting on the floor and trying to kiss the terrier through the chain link, and the terrier was definitely doing her best to stick her tongue through to Sunny's side. I've never gone for sloppy displays of affection like that.

Bill, whom I recognized as a man of decisive action, took control of the situation. "Sunny, remember what we agreed, before we ever left home. One dog only. A big one. And we agreed that we would vote for the best choice."

"I don't care. I want this one," Sunny said. Her bottom lip was beginning to tremble and I could foresee trouble. For the terrier and Sunny, not for me; it was already clear how the voting was going to go.

August 2018

"I don't know why you keep denying it, Sunny," Kelsey said. She was standing in front of the bathroom mirror, experimenting with eyeliner.

"You look gross with all that black junk on your eyes. You look stupid," I told her, which was totally true. Kelsey had overnight turned into somebody I didn't recognize. She used to like to ride scooters around the neighbourhood with me or play video games or just talk about school and stuff, but now all she does is talk to her girlfriends from school about boys. And when they aren't talking on the phone, she's busy texting them. And it's like they can't think of anything to talk about except boys. I was starting to hate her. Oh, and she's started wearing an actual bra too, even though she's still flat as a pancake.

"And for your information," I added, "I'm denying it because I didn't do it. I did not leave the back door open. I don't even use the back door:

you're the one that uses that door because your bedroom is close to it. And I've heard you sneaking out when you're supposed to be in bed."

Kelsey gave me a sideways look when I said that. I hadn't meant to say it, I'd been saving that information for when I needed something from her. Like bringing me back a Frappuccino from Starbucks or doing my math homework for me. I suck at math.

"I always check the door when I enter or exit," Kelsey said. "You know how I am. And you'd better not say anything to Mom or Dad about me sneaking out or you'll be sorry."

It was true about Kelsey checking the door. She had this weird thing she did where she had to turn the light switches off like seventeen times before she left a room. And the same with the doors. She'd open and shut them over and over again, listening for the click of the latch, and pushing to make sure the latch actually had engaged. And windows: she went around the house at bedtime checking every window to make sure they were locked. It drove all of us crazy, and she was seeing a special doctor to try to cure her, but the doctor didn't seem to be helping.

I suddenly felt my eyes burning and I was angry because I didn't want Kelsey to see me cry.

If I still had Teddy, it wouldn't have been so bad that my sister who used to be my best friend was now this weird, mean person who wore bras and makeup and threatened me. But Teddy was gone, and I was alone for the first time in three years. I missed him so much, and every time I thought of his poor mangled bloody body lying in the middle of the street, I just wanted to die, too. I'll never forget the squeal of truck brakes and our neighbor, Miss Adria, screaming. I wish I'd never seen poor old Teddy because now I'll have nightmares about it for the rest of my life.

Everybody says it's my fault Teddy got out, that since Sammy was at soccer practice and Kelsey and I were the only ones home (it was just after school let out and Mom and Dad wouldn't be home for another two hours) that it had to be me who left the back door unlatched, and that's how Teddy managed to be in the middle of the road at the same time that the truck was. But it wasn't my fault. I never touched the back door, but there it was, wide open.

"Aww, Sunny, don't cry," Kelsey said.

"I'm not crying!" I blinked hard and turned away.

"Besides, you've still got Chance—he loves you," Kelsey said. She didn't understand about me and Chance.

"I don't like that dog. I never wanted him in the first place. He's nothing like Teddy." This was true. Teddy was such a sweet boy. He always wanted to be with me and was the most loyal dog ever. My parents agreed to get him for me even though they'd always said we were a one dog family. But for my ninth birthday I'd begged for a miniature poodle. I said that was all I wanted and all I would ever want and if I couldn't have a miniature poodle, then just forget about my birthday because I didn't want anything else. I'd gotten straight A's that year (as usual) and so it was hard for them to say no. So, I ended up with Teddy. And now he's gone, and everybody is blaming me for the accident.

September 2018

Today is Sunny's twelfth birthday. She's been depressed for the last couple months. Ever since the Teddy incident. She won't eat, she says she can't sleep, and she got two Bs on her last report card, which never happens. It was a surprise to me that she took it so poorly. He still had accidents in the house for crying out loud! Anytime he got the least little bit overexcited, there it was, the dreaded yellow puddle. Thank goodness nobody ever thought it was me. Everybody knew how good I am and how mentally challenged Teddy was. Except for Sunny, who adored Teddy and has never quite cottoned to me. I blame the terrier from way back when.

Anyway, like I said, I thought once Teddy was gone, Sunny would finally bond with me. I had hoped. I saw her resistance to me as a sort of challenge. Although I have not given up all hope, I am beginning to wonder if my attempts to win over Sunny may be futile.

And even worse. Earlier today, the unthinkable happened. The worst possible thing. Marjoree and Bill got Sunny another poodle for her birthday. It was a surprise. Sunny actually smiled and laughed for the first time in a long time. She picked up the puppy—a tiny little apricot coloured fluff ball—out of the beribboned box and kissed it. I can't remember Sunny ever kissing me, even though I have faithfully guarded her and her family for years. I didn't say anything, I didn't complain, because as I said earlier, I am a good dog. I lay under the kitchen table and watched it all, though. Watched Sunny lavish affection on that dust ball. Another male too, of course. At least they could have chosen a female puppy, but no, they get this male who will try to challenge my authority.

September 2018

Miss Adria asked to hold my new puppy. I've named him Teddy Deux. I never say the 'Deux' part, which is 'Two' in French (get it? French poodle? Deux?), but just in case Teddy number one is watching somewhere from dog heaven, I want him to know that this dog will never replace him and that I haven't confused them. Teddy One will always have a special place in my heart. I named my new puppy Teddy Deux in order to honour the memory of Teddy One.

"Oh, he's the most adorable thing I've ever seen!" Miss Adria said. "How old is he?"

"He's ten weeks old," I told her. Teddy Deux wriggled in her arms and tried to lick her cheek with his tiny pink tongue. I reached out to take him back. I think this must be what mothers of human babies feel like. It makes me nervous when anyone other than me holds my puppy. I'm afraid they might drop him or something.

"I'm so glad you got another dog," Miss Adria said. "It was so sad what happened to your other poodle; heartbreaking." She glanced at the cars going down our street. "The traffic gets worse every year. I saw the whole thing, you know. It was like slow motion and I wanted to run out and grab Teddy off the street, but it happened so quickly even though it seemed to happen slowly."

I didn't really want to rehash the horrible details of that day, so I just smiled and turned to walk away with Teddy Deux. "At least your other dog, that shepherd—Chance, isn't that his name? —didn't go in the street. He's a smart dog. He and Teddy were both chasing that rabbit, but Chance stopped on the sidewalk and Teddy, well, Teddy didn't.

"Chance? He wasn't outside," I said. Chance had been inside the whole time. At least I hadn't seen him outside when Kelsey and I ran out the front door. He'd been inside later, definitely. And Chance wasn't one to chase things anyway. I decided Miss Adria was mistaken.

Miss Adria frowned. "Oh, well, it looked like him. Anyway, you enjoy your new puppy, Sunny!"

December 2018

In retrospect, it was not the best decision. But at the time it seemed like a good idea. The dog, Teddy One, annoyed everyone in the family (except Sunny) with his constant yapping and his neediness and his incontinence problem. I thought I'd be doing them all a favour. Even Sunny, because I thought without Teddy One in the picture, she would finally come to realize that she didn't need another dog. That one dog, me, was plenty of dog for this family. But I was wrong, and now here we are back in the same exact situation with yet another yapping, little poodle. It would be so easy to let history repeat itself one day while the kids are all in school and Marjoree and Bill are at work. Teddy Deux is locked in a crate when we are home alone because, like Teddy One, he is slow to figure out the concept of doing his business outside and not on the red, antique, Oriental rug in the living room.

Crates are easy to open. Especially if you are outside the crate. I myself have never been put in a crate because I was housebroken at birth. I have never had an accident. And I have never chewed up furniture or shoes - unlike Teddy Deux who has chewed up numerous pairs of shoes and a leather ottoman. Doors are also easy to open. I've watched Kelsey open and shut the back door a million times. I know exactly how to do it. I haven't quite yet decided what the best course of action will be, but I cannot sit by and do nothing as this Teddy Deux destroys the footwear in this household and

ruins all the rugs. I care about my family too much.
I am a good dog.

The Story

***

John Harper

Her storming out was hilarious, but what she said as she left was brilliant.

"If you think you can teach us anything... Your nonsense about plot and narrative – that's not creative writing! That's just copying what everyone has been doing since... well, forever!"

Steve took it pretty well. In fact, he actually said she'd made a good point. I think that's what makes what she said so out of order. We couldn't wish for a better lecturer than Steve. I've been really surprised by quite a few of the units we've covered; I'd say he's actually encouraged us to break most rules. Obviously, it just didn't go far enough for Iesha. I think the final straw for her was when he said it wasn't really a story. Well, how could it be a story? She had literally cut and pasted 10 sentences and phrases from goodness knows where and just put them in any old order. I suppose it was quite interesting in some ways, but it mainly seemed like nonsense. The funny thing is, I think if she'd waited to hear what Steve was actually saying, he was going to say something complimentary about it. Well, it's the only thing she's actually handed in this term, so I reckon he's going to put it in the end of year magazine.

*

Beneath 'The Story', Steve had written a review. He usually only does that for any piece of writing that he admires in some way. I suspect his well-intentioned comments might even be taken as patronising. There is probably some irony here somewhere, but we haven't covered irony yet.

*

"Iesha's story is either an example of incredible laziness, or evidence that she is a true visionary. It took me quite some time to locate the sources of all of the words she used, but it wasn't searching for the quotations that led me to spend more time on her story than the entire body of work from the other students. No, what Iesha has achieved is something quite remarkable, and it is not for me to say whether that is remarkably good, or remarkably otherwise. What at first glance seems like a random selection of famous quotations is in actual fact an invitation to consider the human journey through the words of those who think they made some sense of it. Whether we are much further on in working out the true meaning of life, or can yet say we know the best way to pass our time upon this planet, Iesha points to the fact that it is telling ourselves the story about it that seems to energise us and enable us to press on with our quest. Iesha has succeeded in transcending the rules of writing a short story, and in handing in this one piece of work, without one single sentence of her own, she has argued that there might only be one story after all. It is up to each of you to work it out. — *Excellent work, Iesha!"*

She never came back.

The Prophet Jacksie

***

John Harper

And the Lord caused the prophet Jacksie to rise up in those days....

Clive Staples Lewis (CS Lewis) was born in Belfast in 1898, and at the age of four, his beloved dog Jacksie was killed by a car. The next morning, while out playing with his brother Warnie, three years his senior, they entered the strange and wonderful world of Boxen. They found themselves able to be transformed into animals. Clive Staples was inhabited by Jacksie and ran freely within his new domain.

From this point forward, Clive Staples took on the name Jacksie, which in adulthood became Jack. He was for the rest of his life known by the name Jack, evidencing his childhood brush with the mystical. As happens with so many children, when Warnie left for boarding school in 1905 and approached puberty, he lost his ability to enter Boxen. Jack continued to keep him informed of all that was happening in their other world, but it was only Jack who painstakingly wrote the stories down and illustrated them. Jack was forever able to inhabit more than one world, and wrote many fictionalized versions of his adventures. In the postscript of *Out of the Silent Planet*, published in

1938, Lewis acknowledged his decision to report as fiction the real life events that those without such gifts and experiences would not be able to accept as fact. Warnie was forever torn between his own memories and the 'real' world that denied them.

Jack's journey to Christianity was a complicated one. Interestingly, despite being raised a Christian, Jack became an atheist at the age of 15. The world of Boxen was such an improvement upon the other world that he lived in, that he became increasingly angry with God for creating such a world, and later denied that God could have existed at all. As you might imagine, Jack had a great interest in all things supernatural, and spent a great deal of time investigating the occult and researching many of the stories of ancient Norse, Greek and Irish mythology. These stories which resonated so much with his own experience, made the demands and dry rituals of the Church of Ireland seem even less likely to be anything to do with the True God, the creator of all things bright and beautiful.

Lewis quoted Lucretius as having one of the strongest arguments in favour of atheism:

Nequaquam nobis divinitus esse paratam
Naturam rerum; tanta stat praedita culpa

Which he translated as follows:

Had God designed the world, it would not be
A world so frail and faulty as we see.

As with so many great prophets, it is the journey that proves to be as important as the destination. It was not until 1929 that Jack converted to theism and another two years before he made the full leap towards Christianity as the version of theism that he could finally accept. Interestingly, it was while on a walk to the zoo with his brother Warnie that he made his firm commitment to Christianity. This was the last time that Warnie returned with Jack to the other world of their childhood, and while Jack received the necessary reassurances of his step towards Christianity, Warnie was left as divided as ever.

Jack's work as a prophet began in earnest. Almost everything he wrote after this time was the work of a man who connected two worlds, and sought to bring Christ to every man, woman, and child. He brought Narnia to children as a way of enabling them to sense the real life experiences of his own childhood, and yet because of his post childhood conversion, was able to embed the stories with the Christian message. This would mean that even if a child had some mystical experiences in childhood, but later lost the memory of them, as Warnie had so tragically done, they would find the essence of the magic in the Christian message and their journey to faith would be complete. For those children who have no real life magic in their childhood, the Narnia tales themselves would supply what was needed and would enable a child to find resonance in the true message of Christianity that they could read about by the same author when they moved from his child fiction to his grownup works about Christianity itself. Even those who laughed at the notion of metamorphosed animals, and who had more of a scientific bent, would be helped by the book mentioned earlier: *Out of the Silent Planet*. Purporting to be a science fiction novel and hailed as such, this tale is actually the real life adventure of a man who was kidnapped, taken to Mars and there found extra-terrestrial evidence of the Christian message. However, as with so many of his writings, the messages are oblique and plenty of room remains for the individual to make their own connections and to experience a very personal conversion.

Jack Lewis is the everyman prophet. He put the magic back into Christianity, and almost 60 years after his death, his books still do so. As religions, both Christian and otherwise, falter, and struggle to appeal to this millennial generation, it will be the prophet Jacksie who enables so many more to find their way to faith. He alone will enable many to reconnect the lost mystical memories of childhood with the reality of a world that so often seems bereft of love and kindness.

Garlic Love

***

Theresa Williams

Garlic ice cream was her favorite. She had, after all been born in Gilroy, California, home to Garlic World and the Gilroy Garlic Festival. And, of course, there was the fact that garlic warded off vampires. Her ex-husband was a vampire. She was sure of it, and she ate garlic every day of her life so that he would never return.

> *That vampire had sucked her dry*
> *Left her barren, made her cry*
> *Ran away with the girl next door*
> *Never really liked that whore.*

> *She had called round each day at noon*
> *Songs from the 50s she would croon*
> *Victor then would swing and sway*
> *Till at last he had run away.*

She hadn't suspected that he was a vampire when they first married. He was a software developer. Everyone knew they were pasty white because they spent all their time at their computer. She had been a little creeped out by his excellent Bela Lugosi style accent though, and at Halloween, he really did look the part in that Dracula costume.

He'd been so kind when they first met
She didn't know he was out to get
Her blood, not her heart as she had thought
By his lies she was caught

Shaking her head, she turned around. "Enough of that," she murmured to herself. "What's done is done, and I aim to keep it done, and him out of my life." She had become quite the garlic connoisseur after he left, frequenting the many garlic bars on Main Street. Wine, beer, strong drink. None of it did anything for her.

Give her a Polish white or a Chesnok red
Any kind of garlic went right to her head
She had to be careful on nights like this
When memories turned her resolve to piss.

The problem, she thought, was that garlic kept away more than vampires. The stinking rose, so beautiful in bouquets around her house, for lack of better word, stank. Well, that's what the men said. She thought they were beautiful, and the smell drew her in like a trout on a fishing rod.

Until she met Gary. Gary was a garlic farmer, or was he a rancher?

Garlic is more than a plant I am sure
And my love for Gary is pure
It's not just his garlic that I adore
His stinky breath makes me want more

Victor is gone and that's a good thing
Because now of Gary and garlic I sing
Garlic croissants and clotted cream
Garlic bear claws and garlic ice cream.

Le Rital

***

Maria Claudia Bada

'Tutti hanno guadagnato più di me: l' antiquario Geri, il governo e anche la stampa di tutto il mondo' (Vincenzo Peruggia)

'Io sono un idealista - perseguitato dal numero otto, signor magistrato...' Vincenzo sorrideva, catene ai polsi, affatto preoccupato.

'Le considerazioni le lasci a noi, signor Peruggia. Dunque vediamo, nato a Dumenza l' 8 ottobre del 1881, andaste in Francia nel 1909 e, dopo disparati lavoretti in nero, vi presero in una squadra di imbianchini che aveva appalti al Louvre, vero?'

'Si, tutto sacrosanto, grazie a un diploma di disegnatore di ornato potei lavorare al Louvre'.

'Ma come vi venne in testa di commettere il furto della Gioconda?'

'Prima cosa, credevo che il quadro fosse parte del bottino di Napoleone. E francamente mi si rivoltava lo stomaco a pensare che sto fetecchia avesse rubato la Monna Lisa dalla mia patria. Secondo, io mi volevo solo fare beffe dei francesi che mi ridevano dietro per il mio mandolino e mi chiamavano sprezzanti 'mangia-maccheroni'. *Rital, rital,* mi chiamavano, e ridevano, ridevano come pazzi.'

Fin da scuola da piccolo non aveva avuto molti amici.

Invece di Vincenzo, sarebbe stato meglio essere Robert, Julian, essere un po' più biondo, alto, francomanno. I capelli corvini lo avevano sempre tradito. L'accento era pure buono alla fine, ma nel nome e nella sua pelle scura viveva il ricordo della sua specie. Indelebile.

'Si diceva in giro che avevi un ricco americano interessato alla Monna Lisa,'

'Per carità, magistrato! Nego ogni speculazione del genere, inclusi complici stranieri, eppure vi assicuro che non c'era mica voglia di arricchirsi rivendendo la Gioconda a mercanti disonesti!'

'Tutte fandonie, allora?'

'Tutte favole, signor magistrato, tutte favole! Tanto è vero che la riportai in Italia, la Gioconda, e mi misi subiti in contatto con l'antiquario Geri per riconsegnarla agli Uffizi!'

'Sotto pagamento, però...'

'E certo, mica si fa la puttana per amore di Dio'.

Il processo fu veloce. L'attentato di Sarajevo avvenne nello stesso momento e diede ai giudici una bella spinta a finire tutto e subito. Fu così' che in pompa magna Monna Lisa tornò in Francia e Vincenzo, dichiarato mentalmente minorato, fu spedito in prigione per un anno solo. La patria perdona pure i galeotti se li deve mandare in guerra. Fu così che il povero Vincenzo fu subito arruolato e finì prigioniero.

La notte in trincea arrivavano i ricordi. Lo sgabuzzino dove si era nascosto, il temperino che aveva usato per uscire dal Louvre, gli occhi sbiaditi dalle molte piogge parigine, gli umori del viaggiatore e dell'eroe patriottico finito in gattabuia.

Dopo il conflitto, tornato a Dumenza, dieci anni dopo il famoso furto regalava anche cartoline della Gioconda firmate da lui. La moglie la incontrò così.

'Vincenzo! Quanto tempo! Ma che ci fai qui a Parigi? Non eri stato espulso come indesiderabile?'

'Si, Michele, ma ho fatto un nuovo passaporto col secondo nome, Pietro. Così son rientrato qua con mia moglie. Bella, eh? '.

'Che fessi che sono sti mangiarane! '

E si, tutti gli italiani del quartiere gli volevano ancora bene. Riprese a lavorare, riaccompagnò la moglie a Dumenza per fare nascere la figlia italiana, e rientrò a Parigi.

Un altro 8 ottobre fatale si avvicinava però a Vincenzo. Gli venne incontro a braccia aperte, col sorriso, mentre lui aveva in mano un cabaret di pasterelle e una bottiglia di vino buono. Cadde di botto davanti alla porta di casa. Aveva sempre fatto fessi tutti, ma la triste Signora non la riesci mica a fregare. Mai.

Author Biographies

Renee Schnebelin

Renee Schnebelin lives in Northern Ohio with her husband, three fur babies (Willie, Max, and Danny Cat.), and a Betta Fish named Toby. Renee has always loved to write and has wanted to become a published author since childhood.

She is an Indie RPG girl, growing up playing the original NES, building worlds in The Sims for hours and watching all the TV shows. Probably too much screen time, but it helps her relax in her downtime.

You can find her other works at reneeschnebelin.com.

Ann Powell Lewis

Author Ann Powell Lewis lives in central Mexico with a collection of street dogs and cats, and spends her time writing, reading, and traveling.

Anne-Charlotte Gerbaud

Anne-Charlotte Gerbaud is French but has been living in Ireland for five years. She is passionate, about literature, poetry, theatre, and arts.

Beth Collins

Beth Collins is an actor, theatre-maker and now prose writer! She is pretty new to the writing game, having co-written *'sorry did I wake you'* a play about sisterhood, grief, and the power of bears. This is Beth's first contribution to a literary anthology since primary school, and she is hoping that her parents will be just as proud and provide just as many well-done treats as they did the first time.

Jane Andrews

Jane Andrews is an English teacher and indie author living in Birmingham UK. She writes in a range of genres including YA fiction, fantasy, historical fiction and chick-lit. When she is not writing, she enjoys reading, film and theatre, and long walks with her family.

John Harper

John Harper grew up in the heart of the Sussex countryside, and despite spending many years living in Oxford, Shanghai, and latterly the Auvergne in France, he still considers Sussex to be his home. He has diligently written a journal since he was thirteen years old, and this has enabled him to record the insights and observations he has collected along the way.

He has previously written stage plays but is now writing short stories. He divides his time between teaching, writing, walking, talking, and laughing, as well as enjoying rather a lot of French hospitality. He always tries to look on the bright side no matter what happens, and his writing reflects his pursuit of mindfulness and his great interest in laughter as therapy.

Florence Hood

Florence Hood is a teller of tales, purveyor of doughnuts, and owner of dog. Since her first play was staged in Moscow in 2016, she has published multiple plays, poems, short stories and started the anthology podcast "Once". She loves creating intimate and uncomfortable pieces that aim to stick in readers' throats.

Maria Claudia Bada

Dr Maria Claudia Bada is a trained Sociolinguists specialised in Endangered Languages. A former Researcher, now globetrotter, deeply passionate for environment, photography and sci-fi.

Award-winning blogger and writer, as an artist and a curator she is exploring identity and gender, biodiversity, recycling art, eco-art, landscape change.

Melissa A. Bartell

Melissa A. Bartell, also known as MissMelysse: The Bathtub Mermaid, is a writer, podcaster, improvisor, collector of hats, and rescuer of dogs.

She was on the editorial staff of two now-closed e-Zines: *All Things Girl* and *Modern Creative Life*. She has been published in several anthologies and has published a book of essays: *The Bathtub Mermaid: Tales from the (Holiday) Tub*. Her next book, a collection of horror and fantasy flash-fiction and short-short stories, will be released in October 2020.

You can read and find her current work at MissMeliss.com or listen to it on her podcast at BathtubMermaid.com. Melissa lives in the Dallas-Fort Worth metroplex with her husband and their four dogs, all rescues.

Rebecca Holbourn

Admin for Thirty Stories, Zoom coordinator, always behind the scenes putting out fires and making everyone smile. Usually Rebecca can be found writing scripts and has a true love for theatre and of course Rabbits. Rebecca is our fourteen!

Robert Graver

Robert Graver is an aspiring author making his debut publication within this Anthology. Whilst his stories here are all horror and thriller related, he is aiming to release his debut novel, an Urban Fantasy - Succubus, in the first few months of 2021.

Working for a family owned Sausage Company, Robert writes for two hours a day before each shift, continuously growing and planning his Horror universe, the focus of all his future works. In an attempt to rival the King of Horror himself, Robert has plans and ideas for more than twenty years of stories.

If you enjoyed the shorts in this Anthology, be sure to keep an eye out in years to come for R T Graver.

Samia Nicolas

Samia lives in Hertfordshire, UK, but spent her formative years moving around South East Asian countries with her family, while being fed on a diet of American TV shows and Terry Pratchett books.

She enjoys writing fantasy and supernatural tales, having spent most of her life writing stories, plays and cartoon strips, precariously balancing this with being a science teacher, wife, and mother of one. She is currently working on and hopes to publish a series of urban fantasy mystery novels.

Theresa Williams

Theresa Williams lives in western Washington with her husband, his two cats and her two dogs. Her first love was reading and literature, so consequently she was a librarian for many years.

She is also an earth science geek and can go on for hours talking about volcanoes, earthquakes, geologic history, and plate tectonics. Happily, she now gets paid to do so as a sixth-grade science teacher. For fun (in non-Covid times) she did improv and was just beginning to do theater. Now she is an aspiring playwright.

Thomas Goavers

Thomas Govaers is a theology student from the Netherlands. He's been telling stories for the last six years but wanted to challenge himself by writing it down. As a new writer, he found out writing stories gives him a new way to think about life.